MW01503744

That One Time

The Galeazzi Trilogy

What would you do if the man you're supposed to be spending the rest of your life with is suddenly the devil? When I met Frank, I had thought I'd met the love of my life. I had thought I'd finally found the perfect man. When Frank proposed, I was over the moon.

My world took a nose dive the next morning when I learned that Frank Gala, sexy construction worker, was in fact Francesco Galeazzi, CEO of a multi-million dollar corporation. With some real clear boundaries about Frank's money, I agreed to continue with the wedding plans, hoping I could get used to being married to a man I wasn't sure I ever really knew.

But the world was conspiring against me. Not only did I find myself in a situation I wasn't sure how to handle, but someone had convinced Frank that I was a gold digger. Left out in the cold with a baby on the way, I did the only thing I could do. I began to build a life for me and my child without the father in the picture.

And then the devil came back.

~~~

*Warning: Gay erotic romance. The material in this book contains
explicit sexual content that is intended for mature audiences only. All characters
involved are adults capable of consent, are over the age of eighteen, and are
willing participants.*

Copyright

Table of Contents

That One Time

The Galeazzi Trilogy

AJA FOXX
Copyright © 2022

Chapter One

~ Henry ~

"Will you marry me, Henry?"

My breath caught when I saw the gold ring my boyfriend was holding out to me. We'd only been dating for about six months, but I knew deep in my heart of hearts that this was the man I wanted to spend the rest of my life with.

Frank Gala was everything I could hope for in a husband. He was strong and powerful, a bit overly protective, but he could also be sweet and kind and the gentlest man I had ever met.

It didn't hurt one bit that Frank was totally drool-worthy. He stood just a few inches taller than me, but his sheer presence made him seem ten feet tall. I always felt safe when Frank was around, as if nothing in the world could hurt me. Not even a falling meteor.

His dark brown hair was cut short on the sides and a little longer on top, but it meshed well with the five o'clock shadow he always seemed to have. With the square jaw he sported, it was actually a very good look for him. He looked all business, but also as if he'd just crawled out of bed after a really good night.

It was Frank's deep chocolate brown eyes that really did it for me. When he was angry, they turned as hard as chipped diamonds. When he was happy, they danced. When he was aroused, they melted like molten lava. When they looked at me, they softened.

That might be my favorite.

"Henry?"

"Yes?" I blinked for a moment and realized I had left the man hanging. "Yes, yes, of course I'll marry you."

I'd be stupid not to.

I grunted at the strength of Frank's hug as I pulled me into his arms. Sometimes, Frank was a little stronger than others. I knew it came from working in the construction industry. Frank lifted heavy stuff pretty much all day long, and the thick corded muscles covering his body attested to that.

"We are going to have such a good life, *amore mio*," Frank whispered as he slid the ring onto my finger. It was a simple band, no diamonds or emeralds. Just a never ending circle made of solid gold.

It was perfect.

My brow flickered as I leaned back to look up at Frank. "You speak Italian?"

How cool was that?

Frank grinned. "A little here and there."

I wiggled my eyebrows at him before wiggling my ass over his groin. "That could be fun."

"Keep that up, and I'm going to make love to you."

My heart quickened as I considered the threat. We'd had some pretty heavy make out sessions and a couple of mutual blow jobs, but this was a boundary we'd yet to cross. I had said I wanted to wait. I had to be sure of him.

I was an omega, a rare individual with a genetic mutation, which meant I could get pregnant and give birth. I wasn't about to have sex with anyone I wouldn't be sure would stick around for the long haul. I didn't want to raise a child by myself.

I raised my eyes and met Frank's heated stare. "Okay."

Frank's eyebrows lifted. "Do you mean that?"

I nodded and then gasped when Frank rolled, placing me below him. Frank grabbed my arms, pushing them above my head with one hand as the other skimmed down my side.

I shivered at the contact.

Frank's dark brown eyes were intense as he gazed into down at me. I could see them starting to heat, to turn to molten lava. "Do you want me to make love to you, Henry?"

I swallowed tightly and nodded. I had wanted to be claimed by Frank from the moment I'd laid eyes on the man. I had just wanted to wait until I knew he was with me because he truly cared about me and that this wasn't some one-night stand.

The ring on my finger was all the proof I needed.

"Take your clothes off." Frank's voice was deep, commanding, and guttural.

I couldn't help my trembling as Frank released me. I stood, my hands shaking as I pulled my shirt over my head, tossing it aside, and then pushed my pants down my legs, kicking them off along with my underwear.

I groaned when I bent to remove my socks and felt a hand glide over my ass.

"You have a very sexy body, Henry," Frank said as he stood and slowly started to peel his own clothes off.

I gulped when I saw the large cock slap Frank's belly. My mouth watered to taste it, to take it into my mouth, and suck it until Frank shouted my name.

Frank tossed his clothes aside and then cupped my face, rubbing our cocks together as he kissed me. I moaned when Frank grabbed my ass, pulling me closer, taking the kiss deeper.

My skin broke out in goose bumps as Frank's hands left my ass and slid up my back. I wanted to climb the large man and beg to be fucked.

"I am going to make you mine, Henry. Do you understand this?"

I nodded. "Yes."

A low guttural growl left Frank's lips at my answer.

"Lay on your back," Frank demanded.

I twisted around, scrambling to do as the larger man commanded. I lie down on my back and spread my legs wide. My skin buzzed with excitement at the knowledge that Frank was going to make love to me for the very first time.

"*Bello*," Frank whispered as his eyes roamed over my naked body, but I wasn't sure if Frank was talking to me or to himself. I wasn't even sure what he'd said.

Frank dropped to his knees between my feet and crawled up the mattress, smoothing his hands over my legs. I was dying to move, to wiggle around and beg Frank to fuck me already, but I bit back my words.

My eyes damn near rolled to the back of my head as Frank's fingertips played over my skin, slowly making their way up my thighs toward my aching cock. I almost whined at the slow pace.

Frank wrapped his large hand around my hard shaft. This time, I couldn't stop my moan. I spread my legs wider as Frank stroked my cock. Frank's other hand cupped my balls, massaging them as Frank watched me intently.

I writhed, squirmed, and moaned as I succumbed to the waves of ecstasy that tried to pull me under. I lay there, drowning in a flood tide of exquisite pleasure as Frank took me to another place, a place where I was no longer my own person, a place where Frank owned me, mind, body, and soul.

"Come for me."

My back left the mattress as I cried out, hot jets of cum shooting from my cock as Frank stroked me through my orgasm. The pleasure was pure and explosive. I shouted Frank's name, my head thrashing from side to side. I panted heavily as Frank milked my cock, pulling every last drop from my balls.

"You're beautiful when you come, Henry," Frank whispered. "You make me feel like I could conquer the world."

I licked my lips as I gazed at Frank, wonderment filling me. I watched as Frank swiped his fingers through my cooling seed and then reached below me, circling my hole. At that moment, all I wanted was to feel Frank deep inside of me.

"Frank."

My legs started to shudder as a wet finger entered me and moved around. I hissed when two more fingers entered me a moment later. I bit my bottom lip, pushing back as Frank stretched me. I never knew it could be this good.

It felt fantastic.

"Pull your legs back."

I hitched my hands under my knees and pulled them to my chest. Frank leaned forward, taking one of my nipples into his mouth as he breached my hole again. I reached for Frank's head, grabbing at his hair as Frank stretched me even more.

Frank slid another finger inside of my body as he sucked at my nipple, bringing it to a taut peak. I begged with my body for some sort of release even though I had just come moments ago.

My dick didn't care about that fact.

It wanted more.

Frank nipped at my skin, telling me without words to behave. I released Frank's hair, trying to focus as he inserted another finger. It was hard. I tried, but couldn't focus to save my life.

"I'm going to claim you now, Henry," Frank said as he rose up, pushing my legs farther back as he lined his cock up.

I briefly considered telling Frank that he needed to use a condom, but then I caught the flash of my ring and dismissed it. I loved Frank and he loved me. Whatever happened would happen.

I held my breath and pressed my shoulders into the mattress as Frank plunged into me. Holy fuck! The man was huge. I panted as the sting and bite coursed through my backside, and briefly wondered if this was a good idea.

I curled my fingers into the bedding as Frank began to move. I cried out at the feelings running through my body, threatening to drown me. Nothing had prepared me for this kind of pleasure.

I spread my legs farther apart, wanting Frank to fuck me until I was unconscious.

Frank tucked his body neatly into mine as he grabbed my ankles and lifted my lower body high into the air, assaulting my ass with his huge cock. Frank pulled back and then slammed into my ass, his large cock grazing my prostate as he repeated the move a few more times.

Frank growled as he fucked me harder, deeper, and with more aggression than I had ever imagined was possible. There was no doubt in my mind that Frank was claiming me, placing his ownership over me. I was losing my damn mind and loving it all at the same time.

Sweat trickled down Frank's flawless skin as he hammered into me. Frank growled and dropped my legs, taking my lips in a mind-altering kiss. I wrapped my legs around Frank's waist. Fingers dug into my hips as Frank switched his position, tagging my prostate on every damn stroke. My body buzzed, my heart beating faster as I felt a tingling start in my balls.

"Frank!" I shouted as my orgasm roared up my spine and then down to my groin. My cock erupted, cum splattering everywhere. I cried out, my hole throbbing with my release.

Frank snapped his hips, his cock stretching my ass to the limits. I shouted when Frank's teeth sank into my shoulder. I wasn't sure what was going on, but I prayed Frank didn't stop.

I would die if Frank stopped.

Frank thundered into my ass. I was lost in the feeling of Frank taking me over, dominating me with his body. I shuddered when Frank released my shoulder and threw his head back, roaring out my name. Hot spurts of seed bathed my ass. Frank slammed into me, his fingers digging in so deeply that I knew he was going to leave bruises. I just didn't care.

Frank kissed me before pulling free and falling onto his back. I rolled toward him and then smiled when Frank's arm wrapped around me, pulling me close to his chest. He brushed a kiss over my temple.

"We're going to have an amazing life together."

Warmth spread throughout my entire body. "I think so."

"Close your eyes and rest." Frank's grin was totally wicked. "You're going to need it."

He was right. Frank woke me two more times in the night to love on me. I woke sleepy and a little bit sore, but happier than I'd ever remembered feeling.

"Morning."

I smiled when I turned and found Frank standing in the doorway, a cup of coffee in his hands. "Morning."

Frank's small smile was a little pinched.

"Is something wrong?"

"No, not at all." Frank broadened his smile. "Why don't you jump in the shower real quick and then I'll take you for breakfast."

"Okay," I agreed, but I couldn't help feeling as if something was wrong.

I was hesitant to ask.

When Frank turned and walked back down the hallway, I climbed out of bed and went into the bathroom. My thoughts were turbulent as I quickly showered. I don't think I'd be able to handle it if Frank had changed his mind.

I started to freak out a little, the joy of last night fading. Frank was everything I'd always dreamed of in a man from the time I first realized I liked guys and not girls. He checked every box for me. Every single one.

I didn't want to let that go.

I climbed out of the shower and dried off. The bedroom was empty when I walked back in. I couldn't hear anything in the rest of my small one-bedroom apartment so I hurried through dressing and then walked out to the main room.

"Frank?"

The man was standing at the window with his coffee, staring out to the street below. He turned when I called out to him. I couldn't say his tight expression was welcoming, but it wasn't hateful either.

"What's going on?" I curled my hand into a fist before looking down at the simple gold band on one of my fingers. It was going to kill me to ask, but I had to. "Do you want your ring back?"

"No, no." Frank set his cup down and walked over to draw me into his arms. "No, baby. I put that ring there and that's where I want it to stay."

"Then what's going on? Why are you so upset?"

Frank's heavy sigh did not reassure me.

"I have someone I want you to meet."

"Okay." Frank had never really talked much about his family. I hadn't pushed him to say more than they weren't really in contact. It had seemed too hard for him. I knew what that was like. My family had kicked me to the curb when I came out as gay. I hadn't seen them in almost a decade, and I didn't want to.

Frank cupped my face between his hands. His brow furrowed, his dark eyebrows pulling down deep over his eyes. "I promise I'll explain all of this, Henry, but I just need you to trust me for a little while and not ask any questions. Can you trust me?"

Could I do that?

"Of course I trust you." The answer was simple and immediate. I wouldn't be marrying him if I didn't trust him.

"Thank you," Frank said before brushing a kiss across my lips.

"Does this mean I don't get breakfast?"

Chapter Two

~ Frank ~

This was a big step and I knew it. To say I was nervous was a huge understatement. If Henry refused to sign the papers my lawyer had prepared, there would be no future for us, and that might actually kill me.

It would certainly destroy me.

I'd only known the man for a little over six months, but I couldn't imagine Henry not being a part of my life. I'd learned so much about what I wanted in life from him. He was a simple man who was happy simply being with me.

That was new. I was used to people being at my side because of what I could get them or what they wanted from me. I wasn't used to someone being happy from a simple kiss or cuddle.

Cuddle. That brought on a whole new meaning for me. It wasn't something I had been comfortable with before I met Henry. Now, I couldn't imagine life without it. The simple act of cuddling up on the couch with Henry and watching movies brought me more joy than a trip to Monte Carlo.

"Where are we going?" Henry asked as I led him out of the apartment to the taxi waiting for us.

"No questions, remember?"

Henry frowned, but climbed into the backseat of the cab. I climbed in beside him and gave the driver an address to a building downtown. Henry began to look around as we got underway, but the tight press of his lips told me that he was not happy. I just hoped he trusted me a little longer.

The trip downtown from Henry's one bedroom apartment took a good twenty minutes. Henry didn't say a word and neither did I. He'd have questions and I wasn't ready to answer them. Not yet.

I wish I didn't have to answer them at all, but I would. I owed Henry that much, even if he left me. I just hoped it didn't come to that. If I was lucky, he'd forgive me from withholding this part of my life from him and understand why I had kept things from him.

I had no doubt that he'd be pissed that I had basically lied to him. True, they were lies of omission, but they were still lies, and Henry hated liars.

When we pulled up in front of a tall skyscraper, I swallowed tightly and then turned to look at Henry. "Just a little longer, Henry."

Henry grimaced, but nodded.

I climbed out of the vehicle after giving the driver some money and then held my hand out. Henry got out and took my hand. I saw that as a win so far. I led him into the building and right over to the elevators. I knew exactly where we were going so I didn't need to check in with security.

We rode up to the twentieth floor. When the elevator doors slid open, I led Henry to the reception desk.

Now, for the hard part.

"Francesco Galeazzi to see Mr. Blakely."

I heard Henry gasp even as the receptionist smiled at me.

"Mr. Blakely is waiting for you in the conference room, sir." She got up and walked over to a glass door, pulling it open. "If you'd like to follow me?"

I kept a tight hold of Henry's hand as I followed the woman. She led us down the corridor to a conference room that had a wall of windows on two sides, a large TV screen on another one, and a small side table with a coffee carafe and several cups on the other. A large table and several chairs sat in the middle of the room.

Mr. Blakely stood when we walked in and held out his hand. "Mr. Galeazzi."

"Mr. Blakely, thank you for squeezing us in. I know you have a tight schedule."

"I always have time for you, Mr. Galeazzi."

I smiled before gesturing to the man standing beside me with the confused frown on his face. "This is my fiancé, Henry Warner."

"It's very good to meet you, Mr. Warner," Mr. Blakely said as he shook Henry's hand. "And congratulations on your engagement."

"I'd say thank you," Henry said, "but I'm not exactly sure who I'm engaged to."

Mr. Blakely shot me a frown.

I grimaced, knowing that the time had come to explain to Henry who I really was. "Henry, why don't you sit down so I can explain everything to you?"

"That would be good."

Once Henry sat down, I took the chair beside him. Mr. Blakely took a seat across from the both of us.

"Do you have those papers?" I asked Blakely.

He handed over a stack and a pen. I quickly read through the papers, looking for the one I needed first. When I found it, I slid it over in front of Henry and then held up the pen. "Before I can discuss any of this with you, I need you to sign this. It's a non-disclosure agreement. It means that—"

"I know what a non-disclosure agreement is," Henry said as he took the paper and read it from top to bottom. Once he was done, he held out his hand. I handed him the pen and he signed before pushing them both away. "Now talk."

"My name isn't Frank Gala. It's Francesco Galeazzi."

Henry stared at me.

"Do you understand what I said?" I asked.

"Yes, you just admitted you lied to me and have been lying to me since the day we met."

I winced.

"Yes, that's true." It wasn't like I could disagree with him. I had lied. "But I have a good reason."

"There is never a good reason for lying, Frank." He glared at me. "Sorry, Francesco."

"You can call me Frank." In fact, I preferred it.

"But your name isn't Frank, is it?"

I sighed. This was going to be harder than I thought. "My family is worth quite a bit of money," I started. "When I turned thirty, they started pressuring me to get married and settle down. I was able to put them off for a few years because I needed to help in the family business."

"I take it you're not a construction worker?"

Yeah, there was another mark against me.

"No, not exactly."

Henry crossed his arms and sat back in his chair. His entire demeanor said back off. "Go on."

"So, about a year ago, the pressure got pretty intense. They kept setting me up with blind dates, and their idea and my idea of who I should spend the rest of my life with were totally different."

Henry lifted an eyebrow. "Don't like blondes?"

"Don't like women."

Henry's breath caught. "Do they know you're gay?"

"They know," I said. I'd explained it to them in great detail when I came out at the age of eighteen. "They just believe that it's a phase that I'll grow out of once I meet someone special, so they keep bringing these girls around, hoping one of them will be special."

I was a little reassured when Henry grunted.

"I made a deal with my father. I was going to leave home, and the family business, for one year while I looked for that special someone on my own. If, after a year, I couldn't find someone, I agreed to go home and consider someone they chose."

"Bloody hell, Frank. Why would you do something like that? You'd be miserable."

The outrage in Henry's voice was gratifying and made me smile.

"I was lucky," I said. "Three months into my one-year hiatus, I walked into this little cafe not too far from my work and spotted this gorgeous guy behind the counter. I wasn't stupid. I asked him out on the spot."

Henry stared at me for a moment before glancing away. "Tell me the rest of it."

I sighed again. "So, I meant it when I asked you to marry me, and not because of that stupid deal I made with my father. I honestly do want to spend the rest of my life with you...if you'll have me."

"How do I know you're telling me the truth?" Henry asked. "You've already proved to me that you can lie."

Damn.

I turned my chair to face Henry's and then leaned over to rest my elbows on my knees. My shoulders slumped as I rubbed my hands over my face. Henry was absolutely right. I had no legitimate way of proving I was telling him the truth, not after the way I had lied to him.

"I don't know how to prove to you that I'm not lying, Henry, but I'm not. If..." I swallowed past the lump forming in my throat. "If you want to give my ring back, I'd understand."

"I don't want to give the ring back, Frank, but you lied to me, and not just about who you are." Henry tossed his hands up into the air before standing and starting to pace beside the table. "I don't even know who you are."

"I'm Frank, your Frank. I'm the same man who made love to you last night. I'm the same man who held you in my arms all night long. I'm still me, Henry. I simply have a bit more to my name and my life."

I reached for the other papers Blakely had handed me. "If you sign these, I can show you that life, a life I very much want you to be a part of."

Henry stopped pacing and glanced down at the papers. "What are they?"

"You already signed the NDA. This is the standard pre-nuptial agreement that anyone marrying into my family is required to sign."

"A pre-nup? Jesus, Frank, how much money does your family have?"

"A lot." Millions easily.

Henry held out his hand so I handed him the pre-nup. I was thrilled that he was willing to read it and wasn't tossing my ring in my face and storming out of the room.

"This says the marriage can be ended and I get nothing if I'm unfaithful."

"Yes." I wasn't about to budge on that one. Other parts of the pre-nup were negotiable.

"What about you?" Henry asked. "What happens to you if you're unfaithful?"

"It would never happen, but for the sake of argument, if it did and you couldn't forgive me, then I imagine the marriage would end and we'd go our separate ways."

"I want some changes made before I agree to sign this."

My eyes narrowed. "What sort of changes?"

"I don't want your money, Frank. I never did. If something happens and the marriage doesn't work out, I want nothing from you except what I brought into the marriage." Henry pointed to the paper in his hand. "This five million dollar pay off, take it out. I won't sign if it's in there."

"Henry—"

Henry held up his hand and then set the paper on the table and grabbed the pen. For a moment, I thought he was going to sign, but he crossed out the monetary amount and wrote zero in its place instead.

I was stunned. "That's a lot of money, Henry."

"I don't care. I'm not marrying you for your money."

"No, I understand that." I would be forever grateful for that. "I wouldn't have brought you here and told you all of this if I thought you were, but this money is to take care of you if we ever get divorced."

"We're not going to get divorced so I don't need it."

"Henry—"

Henry held up his hand again. "There is one time where I will take the money. If you are ever unfaithful to me, I want the money when I divorce your ass, and I want ten million dollars. Not a penny less."

Henry wrote that at the bottom of the page and then dropped the pen on the table and handed the paper back to the lawyer. "Have someone type that up and I'll sign it."

"Mr. Warner, as an attorney, I feel I must ask you if you understand what you are agreeing to sign. If you get divorced, except if Mr. Galeazzi is unfaithful to you, you receive nothing, no matter how many years you are married. If you've bought property together, decorated a house, whatever. You will get none of that."

"What about personal items like pictures and such?"

Mr. Blakely glanced at me.

I nodded. "We can write something in there about personal items, clothing, and gifts, stuff like that."

"I just don't want to be standing on the street with nothing but the clothes on my back."

"I can arrange to have a bank account set up for you and put an agreed amount in there every month. No one would have access to it except you. That way, you'd know you'd never be out on the street."

Henry quickly shook his head. "I already told you that I don't want your money. I can earn my own. I want to make sure I can take my personal items if something ever happens."

I hated the idea that Henry was now considering what would happen if we ever got divorced. Now, I suspect, he was always going to be wondering if he was going to have to leave something behind if he ever left.

"You can keep all of your personal items, Henry. You just can't take the company or the family money."

"Unless you are unfaithful to me."

"Yes, unless I am unfaithful to you." I wouldn't be, but he seemed to need that reassurance.

"Fine, then have someone type it up and I'll sign it."

I nodded to Mr. Blakely when he glanced at me. "Write it up as he wrote it."

"One more thing," Henry said. "What about children?"

"You want children I assume?"

We'd never actually gotten around to discussing that.

"I wouldn't mind a couple," Henry replied, his cheeks flushing just a bit.

"Any children that we adopt—"

Henry's eyebrows lifted. "You want to adopt?"

"We could use a surrogate, I suppose. I'm sure my mother would like that." If I provided her with a child, she'd be thrilled, but if I provided her with a blood child, she'd be over the moon.

"So, any children that we adopt or acquire using a surrogate what?"

"They would be raised as Galeazzis."

Henry's eyes narrowed to tiny little slits. "Meaning what?"

"I would retain custody of them if we got divorced."

"No." Henry crossed his arms. "I won't agree to that."

Yeah, I didn't think he would.

"I'm sure we can work out some sort of custody agreement."

"Fifty-fifty."

"Henry—"

There was a thread of steel in Henry's voice when he replied. "What if you decide you want one of those little blondes and divorce me? I'd lose my kids over something I didn't do. No, not going to happen."

"I'm sure we can add something into the custody agreement in case Mr. Galeazzi was unfaithful," Mr. Blakely said.

"There is only one thing in the custody agreement I'll agree to," Henry said. "Any children that we adopt or acquire through use of a surrogate, we share custody fifty-fifty, no matter how the marriage ends. Well, unless one of us starts beating the other or the children or commits a crime."

My parents were going to have a fit, but... "I agree. Type it up, Mr. Blakely."

"Are you sure, sir?" Mr. Blakely asked me. "If you divorce, you'd end up paying a lot in child support."

"No," Henry said, "you can add that in, too. No child support or alimony for either of us."

"You wouldn't want the money to take care of the children?" Mr. Blakely asked.

"I can make enough money to support my kids," Henry said. "They need love and care and support. They do not need trips to the Bahamas."

And that was why I wanted to marry Henry.

Chapter Three

~ Henry ~

It was a good thing that Frank had forgotten to take me to breakfast because I didn't think I'd be able to keep it down. Not only was I still reeling from the knowledge that the Frank I had fallen in love with was some man named Francesco Galeazzi, but now he was taking me to meet his parents.

I was going to be sick.

"Still with me, baby?"

"Maybe."

Frank chuckled. The arm he had around my shoulders tightened and he squeezed me. "The hard part is over. Meeting my parents is easy."

"What if they don't like me?" Considering we came from two vastly different sides of the track, I was pretty sure they wouldn't. I had a job that barely paid over minimum wage. I could not compete with a family who were worth millions.

"My parents are going to love you, and do you know why?"

I didn't have a clue.

"They are going to love you because you make me happy."

I frowned at Frank.

"Henry, my parents married in the old country. They spent their honeymoon on a boat coming to America with my grandmother. When they landed, all they had was a single bag each, the clothes on their backs, and the desire for the American dream. Everything they made came from hard work, love, and the knowledge that family was more important than money."

They sounded wonderful.

I still didn't think they'd like me. I had no real family to speak of and I worked a job at a cafe. Granted, I was putting myself through college one class at a time, but to date, my greatest accomplishment was keeping a roof over my head for the last several years.

"We're here."

My eyes widened and I found it hard to draw air into my lungs.

"Holy shit!"

This wasn't a mansion. It was a palace. Well, maybe not a palace, but close enough. It was huge. I counted four floors just in the main part of the building I could see through the black metal gate. I had no idea how many floors were in the wings on either floor.

"Now, I know it looks big and intimidating, but it's really not."

Wanna bet?

"You have to remember, a lot of people live here. My grandmother, my parents, my younger brother and his husband, and my youngest brother all have rooms here, although Gianni is currently away at the university."

That was not a lot of people.

"We also have a suite of rooms here," Frank continued.

"We do?"

Frank nodded. "If you don't want to live here, I have a place in the city."

"What about that little apartment you have over the bakery?"

"Rented."

"Oh." I had liked that apartment. It was a two bedroom, two bath apartment, and much bigger than mine. It even had a little balcony off the larger of the two bedrooms. Plus, it did sit above a bakery, which meant it smelled fantastic all of the time.

"Am I going to have to quit going to school?"

"No, of course not, but I can pay for your tuition now. You could go to any university in the city and not worry about the cost."

"I'll stay where I am, but thank you." I wasn't about to be accused of being with Frank so he could pay for my education. "I make enough down at the cafe to pay for my tuition."

"Henry, you're barely making ends meet."

Didn't matter. I'd starve before I took money from Frank.

"Is this going to be a problem?"

I snorted. "Probably."

Frank sighed as he sat back in his seat. "Look, I know I kind of blindsided you with all of this, but the pre-nup was not meant for you to think you'd never be able to use my money. It's there in case things go bad between us so you can't demand half my earnings and my family's company."

"No, I get that, but where's the line, Frank? Everyone is already going to look at me as the little gold digger. If I allow you to pay for my education, how is that any better?"

"Because we'd be married," Frank insisted.

"Fine, then we'll wait until we're married." That would at least give me a little time to come to terms with all of this. I was still very uncomfortable with the idea of Frank paying for me to go to the university or just about anything else.

I wasn't sure how I'd feel after we were married.

The taxi stopped in front of a set of steps leading up to a massive wooden door. Frank climbed out and then held his hand out to me just as he had in front of his lawyer's office.

I almost didn't take it.

When Frank's shoulders slumped and he started to lower his hand, I quickly reached out and took it. Once I was standing, I pressed a kiss to Frank's lips. "Give me some time, Frank. This is a lot to take in."

Frank's lips pressed together, but he nodded. "I wish I could have said something to you about all of this before now, but I couldn't."

"I know." I didn't agree with what he'd done, but I understood it from his perspective. Maybe. I'd never had to be wary of having money. "If you lie to me again, we're done. No second chances. Understand?"

Frank nodded again.

I winced when I glanced toward the massive house. "Do you think they're watching us through the curtains?"

The tension in Frank's face faded as he chuckled. "Probably."

Fantastic.

Frank wrapped an arm around my waist and started to lead me up the steps. The front door opened before we reached it. A man in a suit opened the door. "Mr. Galeazzi, welcome home."

"Thank you, Bertram," Frank said. "This is Henry Warner, my fiancé. You'll be seeing a lot of him."

"Welcome, Mr. Warner."

"Henry, you can call me Henry."

"Very good, Mr. Henry."

Yeah, that wasn't much better.

"Are my parents in?" Frank asked.

"Your mother is in the garden with your grandmother. Your father is in his study."

"And the others?"

"Mr. Martino is at the office, Mr. Stewart is still in his suite, and Mr. Gianni is still at the university."

"Thank you, Bertram." Frank started tugging me down the long hallway. "We'll be in my father's study. Can you arrange some coffee and something light to eat in the family dining room? We haven't had breakfast yet."

"Of course, sir."

My jaw was kind of hanging down to my chest so I waited until the butler had walked away before looking at Frank. "You live here?"

Opulent didn't even begin to describe the place. Dark wood crown molding, hardwood floors, a grand staircase, marble tiles, golden framed pictures on the walls, furniture that looked as if it belonged in a museum. It was insane.

"My rooms are a tad bit more modern."

"I hope so."

When we reached the end of the hallway, Frank knocked on a set of double doors.

"Come," someone from inside called out.

Frank opened the door and ushered me inside. There was an older man sitting behind the desk who looked a lot like Frank. He was just as tall, but a little rounder and he didn't have the same scruff on his face that Frank had. It was a well groomed mustache, though.

The man smiled as he stood. "Francesco, *sei a casa*."

"*Ciao*, Papa." Frank smiled. "I am home, and I've brought someone with me for you to meet. This is my fiancé, Henry Warner."

The man's bushy eyebrows lifted. "Your fiancé?"

"We've already been to see Blakely, and Henry signed all the necessary papers, but only after he put me through the ringer."

I elbowed Frank in the side and whispered out of the corner of my mouth, "Don't tell him that. He's going to think I'm a gold digger."

Frank chuckled. "There was a bit of negotiating before Henry would agree to sign the pre-nup." Frank reached in his pocket and pulled out a copy of the prenuptial agreement I'd signed and then handed it over to his father.

The man frowned as he glanced down and read the paper, but after a moment, he glanced up. "You refused a divorce settlement?"

"Yes, unless Frank is unfaithful to me."

"Why would you do this? It's a lot of money. If things end badly, you'll have nothing."

I shrugged. "I have nothing now. How would that be any different?"

"Henry works at a cafe while putting himself through school at the university," Frank said. "That's where we met."

"Francesco will pay for your education. You don't have to work at your cafe anymore."

"No, thank you," I said firmly. "I can put myself through school, and I'm not quitting my job."

I wasn't even sure I was giving up my apartment. Not yet.

"Son—"

"You can see from the prenuptial agreement I signed that I'm not after Frank's money. Until this morning, I didn't know he had any." I jabbed my elbow into Frank's side again when he grunted. "I didn't even know his name wasn't Frank."

The man's eyebrow quirked up as he glanced at his son. "You did not tell your fiancé what your real name was?"

I knew Frank was rolling his eyes even if I couldn't see him. "I accepted Frank's marriage proposal last night when I thought he was nothing more than a construction worker living in a small apartment above a bakery." I waved my hand to encompass the large office. "All of this? This is going to take some getting used to."

"So, that is what you have been doing with yourself."

I raised my eyebrows in surprise. "You didn't know?"

"He would not let me or his mother visit and only came home once a week to attend church with the family and then have dinner."

I turned and glared up at Frank. "That's why you were always busy on Sundays?"

It had bothered me for the longest time, but Frank had sworn up and down he was following his family traditions, and he wasn't quite ready to tell me what those traditions were or allow me to join him.

"I thought we'd covered all of the things you lied about. Are there more?"

"No, I promise."

"And how much is your promise worth?"

The laughter coming from behind me was even more surprising than Frank not telling his family what he'd been doing. I turned to look at the man. He was holding his hand out to me. I was hesitant, but for the sake of diplomacy, I reached over and shook it.

"I am Bellino Galeazzi, but you can call me Papa. Welcome to the family." He waved his hand to a brown leather chair by his desk. "Please, come sit and tell me what this *idiota* has been up to."

I shot Frank a hard stare before walking over to sit down where Bellino had indicated. I crossed my legs and clasped my hands together in my lap, hoping no one would see them shaking.

I was still a little wigged out.

"So, how did you meet my son?" Bellino asked.

This time, when I looked at Frank, I had a smile on my face. "Him and a bunch of the construction crew from the building down the street came in for lunch. After I took his order, he asked me out."

Frank chuckled. "And you refused. I had to eat there for two weeks before you'd even agree to go out for coffee with me."

Bellino was all smiles. "*Bene, bene,* you did not make the chase easy for him."

"He was brutal, Papa."

"I was busy putting myself through school," I argued. "I didn't need some hot Italian construction worker messing that up."

"After he finally agreed to go out with me, he was still brutal. He insisted we go Dutch even when I invited him out, and half the time, he wanted to eat in instead of going out or to make food at home and take it with us."

I felt the heat in my cheeks and knew I was blushing. There was nothing I could do about it. There had been times when Frank had argued with me about not just going out, but I had stuck to my choice and I still would. His money was not going to change that.

"Sounds very reasonable," Bellino said. "Your mother makes quite the picnic lunch. I remember many a times when she would make us a picnic to take to the park. You and your brothers loved it."

Frank grinned. "Yes, it was fun."

I smacked Frank on the arm since I couldn't get him in the gut with my elbow. "Then why did you argue with me about it?"

"Because I'm an *idiota.*"

Chapter Four

~ Frank ~

I turned when the door opened and then smiled and stood up when I realized it was my mother. I wrapped my arms around her and gave her a big hug. I hadn't realized until that moment how much I missed her. Weekly visits were just not enough.

"Ciao, Mama, mi sei mancata."

"Francesco, you're home." She cupped my cheeks between her hands and stared up into my eyes as if looking for something. I don't know if she found it or not, but she smiled at me. "Are you home to stay?"

"I'm working on that." I reached down and took her hand and then led her over to Henry. "Mama, this is Henry Warner, my fiancé. Henry, this is my mother, Delinda Galeazzi."

Henry stood up and held out his hand. "How do you do, ma'am?"

I didn't think Henry would believe me in that moment, but the scary one was actually my grandmother. She might be in her mid seventies, but she was still a force to be reckoned with. She had been born at the tail end of World War II and had to grow up in an Italy that had been first ransacked by the Nazis and then practically leveled by the Allied Forces.

Somewhere along the way, she'd met my grandfather, gotten married, and started a family. She lost her husband and two sons to what Italians call the Years of Lead, the time from late 1960s until the late 1980s. It was a period of great economic crisis, widespread social conflicts and terrorist massacres carried out by opposing extremist groups. It was also why my family had immigrated to the United States.

It had given Eva Galeazzi a strong sense of right and wrong and an unbreakable love for her family, which was one of the reasons we all lived in the same house together. None of us had the desire to break her heart. It was also the reason I hoped Henry would agree to live here.

My mother made a tsking noise as she circled Henry. "You need to eat more. You look like you are starving to death. There is no meat on your bones. Who is taking care of you?"

"Um." Henry glanced at me with a deer in the headlights look. "I take care of myself."

"Where is your mama, Henry? Why is she not caring for you?"

I cringed. "Mama, maybe—" I snapped my lips together when she raised her hand. I might want to save Henry, but I liked my head attached to my shoulders.

I heard Henry swallow hard.

"My mother didn't want me anymore after she learned that I was gay, none of my family did."

My mother gasped, but I expected nothing less from her. I smiled when she started swearing in Italian, grabbed Henry's head, and pulled it to her chest as she hugged him. I let it go on for a moment before reaching for Henry and dragging him into my arms.

I didn't expect him to slap my arm and push away from me, going right back to hugging my mother. He glared at me over my mother's shoulder. "Do you know how long it's been since I've had a mom hug?"

"I will give you a mom hug whenever you want one, *bambino*."

Pretty sure I just lost my fiancé to my mother.

"Can we move this to the family dining room, Mama?" I asked. "Henry hasn't had breakfast yet and I asked Bertram to arrange something for him."

"Oh yes, of course." Mama flashed Henry a bright smile as she patted his hand. "You just come with me, young man. I'll get you fattened up in no time."

I chuckled and shook my head as my mother led Henry out of the office. I turned when my father patted me on the shoulder. "You might get him back in time for the wedding, but I make no promises."

"Yes, I'd had the same thought."

"What happened to Henry's family? I assume you had them investigated."

I nodded because I had. "They kicked Henry out when he was sixteen years old, the moment he told them he was gay. He's never spoken to them again. Everything he has, everything he's accomplished since then, is all due to his hard work."

"I can understand why he doesn't want you paying for his education then. He sounds quite independent."

"He is, and I love that about him, but I also foresee issues with it. Since this morning when he learned who I really was, if I even mention money, he gets upset."

"Hmm, while that bodes well in some incidences, it does not in others. He will have to grow used to having money, son. You know this."

"I know. I'm hoping to ease him into it."

"Good luck with that. If I know your mother, she's going to start planning the wedding immediately, and it won't be a little affair. Her oldest boy is getting married. She's going to want to celebrate that in a big way."

That's what I was afraid of.

"As long as Henry gets the wedding he wants, I don't care what she does."

My father patted my shoulder again. "That's the spirit."

I followed my father out of his office and down the hallway to the family dining room. It was smaller and more intimate than the large formal dining room. This is where we ate when we were together as a family.

I walked over and pressed a kiss to my mother's temple and then Henry's before taking a seat beside him. I eyed the plate before him. Bertram and Mrs. Rovito, our cook and housekeeper had come through for me. Henry was enjoying Eggs Benedict, which was one of my favorite breakfast foods. I also noticed a bowl of fresh fruit and a glass of orange juice sitting in front of him.

I poured myself some coffee and then grabbed a piece of toast to munch on as I listened to my mother and Henry talk. The conversation was mostly about food, but also things that Henry liked, his favorite colors, his favorite flower...basically wedding stuff.

"Mama, give the man some time to eat before you hit him with wedding plans."

Henry's fork dropped to his plate. He looked up at me with wide eyes. "We were talking about the wedding?"

I smiled.

"Can't we just be engaged for awhile?"

Wait.

I frowned. "How long is awhile?"

Henry shrugged. "I don't know. A couple of months or so?"

"Oh, baby, we're going to be engaged for at least a year. It'll take Mama that long to plan the wedding."

I was not happy when Henry's shoulders slumped as if a great weight had been lifted from them. "We can get married earlier or later, whichever. We simply need to decide on a date."

"Two thousand and twenty five sounds good."

I chuckled nervously. Surely he didn't mean that?

"How about July of next year?" I countered. "That's over a year from now. That should be plenty of time for you and Mama to plan the wedding."

The tension went right back into Henry's shoulders. "I'm supposed to plan the wedding? I don't know anything about planning weddings. And what about my work and school?"

"That's why we have Mama. She'll take care of all the details. You just have to tell her what you want."

"I don't suppose we could elope?"

"No."

"Yeah, I didn't think so."

Henry hadn't picked up his fork again so I reached over and grabbed his hand and brought it to my lips. After placing a kiss on it, I held it to my chest. "This isn't something scary, Henry."

Henry snorted. "Says you."

God, I adored him.

"It's really not. It's simply not something you're used to. By the time the wedding gets here, you'll be fine."

Henry's eyes narrowed. "You'd better not be lying to me again."

I held up my hand, my fingers straight up and my thumb folded in against my palm. "I promise."

"When did you lie to this lovely *bambino*, Francesco?"

"Uh..."

Henry chuckled as he picked up his fork and began telling my mother all about it. From the glares I was getting, I'm pretty sure I had some serious kissing up to do.

"Papa, can I have Grandfather's ring?" I asked. "I'd like to give it to Henry instead of the ring I gave him." As the oldest child, it had been promised to me in my grandfather's will.

Henry's head snapped around. "You're not taking my ring."

"Henry, that's just a gold band. My grandfather's ring is much—"

Henry held up the hand his engagement ring was on. "This is the ring you put on my finger when you proposed to me. This is the ring I'm going to wear."

"Oh, I like this boy," my mother said.

I really wanted Henry to wear my grandfather's ring. "Would you consider wearing both? This is my grandfather's ring. It was given to me to give to the man I married."

Henry grimaced. "Fine, I'll wear it." Henry held up his hand again. "But this is my engagement ring and it will be my wedding ring when we get married."

I didn't like it, but I'd take it.

"Father, could you get the ring?"

Bellino nodded before standing up. "I've had it in the safe since you left nine months ago. I was hoping I wouldn't need to return it to the vault."

Henry leaned over to me and whispered. "Vault?"

"Bank vault, baby. We don't keep stuff like that just lying around the house. Too many chances of getting robbed. We keep all the important stuff in the bank vault."

"Ah," Henry said, but I could tell he had no idea what I was talking about.

He would.

When my father came back, I smiled as I took the black velvet bag he held out to me. I opened the end of it and dumped the ring out onto the palm of my hand. I felt almost giddy when I held it up for Henry to see.

"This was my grandfather's ring. Grandmother worked for an entire year to pay for the gold and the engraving. At the time, she couldn't afford real diamonds so she had zirconium chips put in it. Over the years, one at a time when each of her children was born, she'd buy another diamond and have it put in the ring."

"It's beautiful," Henry whispered.

"My mother always said that she and Papa were the leaves that held the ring together," my father said, "but the diamonds, one for each of their children, were what made it truly shine."

Henry gulped and his eyes rounded. "Those are real diamonds?"

"Five diamonds, a total of twelve carats, all set in fourteen carat gold. Here, let's try it on." I reached for Henry's hand again and then slowly slid the ring down his finger. It was a little big. It kind of spun around Henry's finger. "We might need to get it sized."

"What if I lose it?"

"You won't." I was sure of it. Henry would hold onto both those rings until the day he died. The gold band, because that was the ring I had given him when I proposed, and my grandfather's ring because of how special it was to me.

"Yeah, but—"

"I have faith in you, baby."

"Good morning, family."

I briefly closed my eyes and drew in a breath before opening them and turning to look toward the doorway. I was not a huge fan of my brother-in-law. He seemed to make my brother Martino happy, which was the only reason I tolerated the man.

"Good morning, Stewart."

"Francesco, you've returned. Just dropping in for a visit or...?"

"I came home to introduce Mama and Papa to my intended."

Stewart's eyes snapped to Henry. "You're engaged?"

"I am." I smiled as I lifted Henry's hand and pressed a kiss to the inside of his palm. "This is Henry. We've set the wedding date for July of next year so he and Mama have plenty of time to plan our wedding. I'm sure it will be spectacular."

I knew it was wrong of me to needle Stewart, but I'd always felt as if he had trapped my brother into marriage. Stewart was an omega who had become pregnant while dating Martino. Their wedding had been a hurried affair and not the big elaborate wedding I knew Mama was going to plan for me and Henry.

Unfortunately, Stewart had miscarried, although I had my suspicions that he'd never been pregnant in the first place. It seemed a little too easy to me that he had miscarried just as soon as the ink was dry on his marriage contract.

His marriage to my brother was one of the reasons the family had started requiring a pre-nuptial agreement, not to mention the non-disclosure agreement. None of us were willing to let some little gold digger come in and take what my parents had worked so hard for.

Still, I did need to keep the peace, for my brother's sake if nothing else.

I smiled and waved him over. "Would you like to join us?"

Stewart walked over and took a chair across from me and Henry. He poured himself a cup of coffee and then sat back in his chair. The smile on his lips didn't quite reach his eyes as he focused on Henry.

"Engaged, huh? This seems rather sudden. I didn't even know you were seeing anyone, Francesco."

"Henry and I have been dating for six months." I grinned at Henry as I grabbed his hand and brought it to my lips. "He finally agreed to marry me last night."

Henry's quiet chuckle was almost drowned out by Stewart's gasp.

"Is that your grandfather's ring?" Stewart asked.

I frowned as I glanced at the man. "It is."

"Martino promised it to me."

My eyebrows shot up in shock, but only for a second before pulling down low over my eyes. "Martino had no right to do that. The ring doesn't belong to him. It was left to me by my grandfather to give to my intended."

Stewart's eyes darted to my mother and father before moving back to me. He plastered a smile on his face that was so fake, it was practically plastic. "I just meant that Martino said I could have it if you didn't get married since you kept turning down the women Mama and Papa wanted you to marry."

"Even if I never got married, you would not be getting that ring, Stewart. It belongs to me." It grated on my nerves that he ever thought he had a chance at getting it. I don't even know how he knew about it. I'd certainly never told him, and I doubted Martino had either.

If he had, we'd be having a conversation about that.

I smiled, but it was just as fake as Stewart's smile. "I'm sure Martino can buy you some other pretty bauble."

I grunted when Henry's elbow jabbed into my side.

Chapter Five

~ Henry ~

I was so tired, my hair follicles hurt. I knew a majority of it was due to the stress of my day. First finding out that my fiancé was not who I thought he was, then those stupid pre-nup papers, and then meeting Frank's family.

I was ready for this day to be over.

I finished drying my hair and then dropped the towel on the bed beside me and glanced around Frank's bedroom. He was right. His suite of rooms was much more modern than the rest of the house.

My jaw had practically become unhinged when I'd first walked in. For some reason, I had thought Frank's place would be all black and chrome or something. It wasn't.

The main room of the suite was a large living room area complete with floor to ceiling windows and double doors leading out to a balcony, a fancy fireplace that looked as if it was made out of knotty pine wood and a white stucco material, and a very large white sectional sofa. The sofa was big enough for both of us to stretch out on and still have room left over. What wood there was in the room—coffee table, side table, built in bookshelves, etc—were all a nice knotty pine color. There was even a colorful rug in the middle of the floor.

Frank had shown me the spare bedroom, his study, the guest bathroom, a small kitchenette, the master bedroom and en-suite bathroom.

I was in love with that bathroom. The large shower alone could convince me to move into the mansion. It was big enough for four people to shower at the same time and had multiple showerheads, including a rain showerhead hanging right in the middle of the tiled shower stall.

I'd enjoyed every second of my shower.

I glanced up when the bedroom door opened and Frank walked in. "Hey."

Frank smiled at me as he started stripping off his clothes. Watching him undress was amazing. It was like Christmas morning opening all my presents, one at a time. Only, I was watching Frank's sexy body being revealed, one item of clothing at a time.

"I see you enjoyed the shower."

"Maybe."

Once Frank was naked, I inhaled a shaky breath. He was built very well.

Frank cocked an eyebrow at me before shaking his hips back and forth, making his hardening cock dance.

I burst out laughing.

Frank grinned and walked over to stand in front of me. All laughter left me as my level of lust went from semi interested to automatic overdrive. Frank was damn sexy, even more so knowing that he belonged to me.

"God, you're hot!"

Frank grinned down at me. "Yeah?"

I rolled onto my hands and knees and moved to the edge of the bed. I eyed the nice thick cock bouncing in front of my face, licking my lips.

"Oh yeah," I whispered right before licking the tip of Frank's cock.

The low, needy groan I heard from above made me feel almost giddy. I loved making Frank feel good. It was almost as good as an orgasm, almost. Nothing on earth really topped having an orgasm created by someone who cared about me.

"Fuck, baby, you're so good at that," Frank groaned. "Your mouth is like magic."

I grinned around the cock in my mouth before swallowing more of Frank's large shaft. The soft skin over hard steel, the sweet taste of pre-cum, all of it combined to drive me crazy.

My cock was so hard, I thought I might burst. When Frank growled, it sent shivers of delight down my spine, making me even harder. Frank pushed me back onto the bed and grabbed the bottle of lube off the nightstand. He poured some out onto his fingers before dropping the bottle onto the mattress.

The level of heat arching between us could have started a forest fire. I wrapped my arms around Frank as the man settled over my body. I loved the feeling of being weighted down. It let me know I was being loved on.

"I hope you're ready for me," Frank said as two lubed fingers pushed into my ass.

I hissed at the sudden intrusion burning, aching. My hips bucked, driving Frank's fingers deeper inside my clenching grasp. The burn slowly dwindled away as Frank thrust his fingers in and out, to be replaced by a deep ache.

"You like that, baby?"

I panted. "It...It would be better if it were you." My voice sounded low and deep, needy.

"Soon, Henry," Frank said. "I just have to stretch you out a bit more before you can take me."

No matter how much I wanted to feel Frank plunge into me right that second, I knew Frank was right. The man was hung like a horse. I could be seriously injured if Frank didn't prepare me properly first.

But once he did...

"More, Frank," I begged. My fingers clawed at the sheets for a moment before I gripped my thighs above my knees and pulled them up to my chest, spreading my legs as far apart as I could. I knew I looked wanton. I just didn't care.

A third finger pushed into me. It was quickly joined by a fourth finger. My mind slid into a haze of lust. When Frank's fingers began gently tugging at my nipples, Frank's lips devouring me, I started shuddering.

My orgasm wasn't far off. "Frank, if you don't get that beautiful cock in my ass in the next two seconds I'm going off without you."

I narrowed my eyes when Frank chuckled. It was an evil sound. I groaned in protest when Frank pulled his fingers away until I felt a small slap to my hip. I raised an eyebrow at Frank.

"Roll over, baby," Frank commanded. I couldn't roll over fast enough. I pushed myself up onto my hands and knees and presented myself to Frank. I wiggled my ass in anticipation. The wait was half the fun.

I inhaled sharply a moment later when I felt the head of Frank's cock press against my tight entrance. Frank seemed to want to tease me, pushing in just a little, but never fully breaching me. I groaned and then clutched the sheet in my hand and gritted my teeth.

"Frank!" I wailed. Begged. Pleaded. Prayed. "Please."

The large mushroomed head pushed in. Frank moved so slowly I thought I might die of old age before I was fully impaled on the man's cock. Deciding to take matters into my own hands, so to speak, I braced myself then pushed back with all of my strength.

The intrusion was swift, hard, and I loved every second of it, especially when Frank's groan rang out from behind me as the man sank all of the way in. I could feel Frank's hips press against me, his hands gripping me with unnatural strength.

"Fuck, Henry, why'd you do that?" Frank groaned as he began thrusting into me with deep, powerful strokes. "Now I can't go slowly."

"Didn't want slowly," I breathed out between grunts. "Want you to fuck me so hard I can't walk for a week."

"You're wish is my command, baby." Frank leaned over me until his body blanketed me and then he began moving, thrusting into me.

"Oh, god, I hope so," I whispered. I gripped the headboard in front of me, my knuckles nearly white. The feeling of Frank thrusting into me with all the force behind his sexy body nearly undid me.

"You like that, baby?" Frank asked. "You like my cock in your ass?"

"Yeah," I panted. I worked on squeezing the inner muscles that gripped Frank's cock, smirking when I heard the man groan, the rhythm of his thrusts becoming erratic. "Harder, Frank."

"My ass," Frank growled. "My pace."

I yelped as Frank's thick hand came down on my ass several times. It made my cock even harder. I thought I might explode any minute. I reached my hand under my body and grabbed my own cock, holding it tightly.

The friction of my cock sliding through my hand with every powerful thrust of Frank's body quickly had me on the edge of a magnificent orgasm. I could feel it coming, feel my balls tighten up getting ready to explode.

"Frank!" I wailed.

"I'm right there with you, baby," Frank replied. "Come for me, Henry, come all over my cock."

I cried out, Frank's simple words enough to send me over the edge. My body shuddered as my orgasm grabbed me, white pearly seed shooting all over the sheet beneath me.

I distantly heard Frank bellow behind me. Fingers dug into my hips as Frank thrust heavily into me, spurts of the man's release filling me before Frank collapsed down over the top of me.

Frank rolled us to our sides, cuddling me in his arms. I felt each caress of the man's hands as the loving gestures they were meant to be. I wiggled back against the bigger body behind me, content to lie in Frank's arms for now.

"Don't you think we should get up and clean up a bit?" Frank asked after a moment, wiggling my hips a little, reminding me that he was still buried deep inside of me.

"Nope." I chuckled. "I'm pretty happy right where I am."

"We will have to get up at some point. We're expected at dinner at six."

I glanced at the clock I'd spotted on the nightstand earlier. "It's only two o'clock now. We've got time."

Besides, I needed a little space from everything, even if it was only a little while. I was feeling very overwhelmed at the moment. "I'm in love with your shower. I may demand that be put into the pre-nup."

"Nope, you already signed. If you want the shower, you're going to have to stay married to me."

I sighed loudly. "If I must."

Frank growled. I laughed as he rolled me under him and pinned my hands above my head. I could see the laughter in his eyes slowly fading as he grew serious.

"How are you handling all of this?"

"I think I'm still trying to take it all in."

"Is there anything I can do to make it easier for you?"

I shook my head. "No, I don't think so. I just have to wrap my head around it, you know? I dreamed about what life would be like with you many times, but I never imagined this."

Frank winced so I reached up and stroked my hand down the side of his face before cupping his cheek. "I didn't say it was a bad thing. Just that I need to change my way of thinking. I imagined us living in one of our apartments and slowly saving up the money to buy a house and build a family together. This"—I waved my hand around—"never even entered my mind."

Frank dropped down onto the mattress next to me again. "It's not all bad, you know. There are a lot of things this life can bring us."

I rolled onto my side to face Frank. I could see that he was really trying and wanted to make him feel better. "Oh yeah? Like what?"

"Have you ever thought of going horseback riding? We have horses in the stables out back and about five miles of trails in the woods beyond the stables."

I lived in the city so I never really thought about it, but I could see where that could be a draw. "I'm listening."

Frank chuckled. "Well, we can honeymoon anywhere in the world you want to go. We can even visit several different places." Frank traced over my lips with the tip of his finger. "I'd love to show you the old country where my family is from, and then take you to Florence and Rome, maybe Paris or London."

"I'd love to see where your family is from." I wasn't sure about the rest of it, though. Dreaming about visiting exotic locations around the world was a bit different than actually seeing them. I'd hate to be disappointed and have my fantasies ruined.

"If we live out here, I'll be getting you a car so you can get back and forth to school."

"I don't need a car, Frank."

"Actually, you do. It's too expensive to pay for a taxi every day. A car is cheaper solution."

I hated that that made sense. "Okay, I'll consent to a car, but nothing fancy. I just need something that runs well and has good gas mileage."

"I was thinking of a 2021 BMW 8 Series 840i Convertible in Blue Ridge Mountain metallic blue with ivory white interior."

I narrowed my eyes. "You already bought it, didn't you?"

Frank's cheeks flushed. "Last week."

I laughed because I had no other choice. If I didn't, I'd cry. "Frank, I don't need you to buy me an expensive car."

"It has a very good safety rating as well as being sporty and luxurious. It's supposed to be really nice for long drives."

"My school is only twenty minutes away."

"True, but the cottage by the sea that I bought for you as a wedding present is three hours away, so having something to make the drive easier would be nice."

I lifted myself up onto my elbow. "You bought me a cottage as a wedding present?"

"I figured there would be times when we would need to get away from all of this and have it be just the two of us so I found a place on the lake big enough for you and me." Frank shrugged. "And maybe a kid or two and a dog."

I stared for a moment before laughing and dropping back down onto the mattress. "You're too much, Francesco Galeazzi."

"Too much? Is that a bad thing?"

"No." I pressed my hand against Frank's chest and spread my fingers over his skin. "Like I said, I just have to wrap my head around it."

Frank pressed my head down to his chest. I shuddered when he threaded his fingers through my hair. That really felt good.

"The cottage and the car are in your name," Frank said. "They're both paid off so you don't have to worry about making payments or anything."

"You put them in my name?"

"They're yours, gifts from me. Of course I put them in your name. If they were gifts to me, I would have put them in my name."

That made sense, but it also made me very uncomfortable. "When we get married, I want them in both our names. I don't want anything that isn't yours, too."

Frank's happy grin made all of this worth it.

Chapter Six

~ Henry ~

I didn't have class today, but I did have a lot of homework, which meant sleeping in was not a luxury I had. I needed to get home to where my laptop and study material were. It wouldn't hurt to take a shower and put on a change of clothes either.

I tried not to wake Frank as I climbed out of bed, grabbed my clothes, and hurried into the bathroom. I took care of my morning stuff, brushed my teeth and hair, and then got dressed.

Once I was all done, I walked out of the bathroom, grabbed my shoes, and then made my way out of the bedroom. I put my shoes on in the living room before looking for a pad of paper and a pen. I wanted to leave Frank a note so he'd know where I went.

I couldn't find one so I thought I'd find the butler guy and ask him to give Frank a message for me. I could also call him later, once I knew he'd gotten up. I just didn't want him to worry when he couldn't find me.

Besides, it was the polite thing to do.

It was still fairly early so I tried to be quiet as I let myself out of Frank's suite and then made my way down the grand staircase to the first floor. I looked around a bit, but couldn't spot anyone. Maybe I was the only one up?

I started walking through the rooms looking for someone, anyone. When I reached a set of large glass doors that opened out into what looked like an inside garden, I paused to take it all in. Greenery and flowers hung from every available spot. The walls of the structure were all made of large glass panels.

"Well, don't stand there, young man, come in."

I froze as my eyes rounded. I didn't see anyone, but I know someone had spoken to me. "Hello," I called out tentatively.

"How do you take your coffee?" the mysterious someone asked. "I like mine like we had it in the old country, strong, with just a hint of sweet cream."

I stepped into the room and started walking through the thick foliage. When I reached the other side of the room, it opened up. I found an older white haired woman sitting at a small patio set in front of French doors that were open, letting in the morning light. The sight of the manicured grounds and then forest beyond was breathtaking.

"Sit down."

"Yes, ma'am." I quickly took my seat.

"Coffee?"

"Please."

She grabbed an extra cup—I didn't think about it until later, but there were only two cups. Mine and hers—and then poured me some. After she handed me the filled cup, she gestured to the two jars on the small tray. "There is sugar and creamer if you take it."

"Thank you." I put a little sugar in my coffee and a lot of creamer. I almost groaned when I took a sip. "This is good coffee."

"My sister ships it to me from the old country. The stuff they have here is weak."

I wouldn't know.

"So, you think you are going to marry my grandson."

Oh god.

I thought about my reply for a moment before admitting, "Well, he did ask me."

The old woman snorted.

I didn't know whether to be impressed or outraged.

"Did you sign that ridiculous piece of paper?"

I quickly frowned. "The pre-nuptial agreement?"

She snorted again.

"Yes, I did, but I understand why Frank had it. He wants to make sure everything his parents worked for isn't lost if we get a divorce."

"Do you plan on getting a divorce?"

"Only if Frank is unfaithful to me, and then I get ten million dollars."

That seemed to gain her interest. She lowered her cup and sat up a little straighter. "I've seen the pre-nup and you received five million if you got divorced, nothing if you were unfaithful. I don't remember there being a clause in there for Frank being unfaithful."

I shrugged. "I made the lawyer change it before I agreed to sign it."

"What other changes did you make?"

"If we get divorced, except if Frank is unfaithful, I leave the marriage with what I came in with. Nothing more, nothing less. If I am unfaithful, I get nothing. If Frank is unfaithful, I get ten million dollars. If we adopt any children or use a surrogate, we share custody fifty-fifty. There will be no child support or alimony for either of us."

The woman stared at me for the longest time before smiling and reaching over to pat my arm. "You'll do, son. You'll do."

I had no idea what that meant.

"Who are you?"

"I am Eva Galeazzi, Bellino's mother. You may call me *Nonna*." She pointed to the ring on my finger; the one Frank had given me yesterday. "That was my husband Arturo's ring."

"Oh, I'm sorry. Do you want it back?" I started to pull the ring off, which was easy because the thing just spun around my finger. We really needed to see about getting it resized, or maybe I could wear it on a necklace or something. I really didn't want to lose it.

"No, it's where it's supposed to be. My husband wanted our firstborn grandson to have it to give to the one he intended to marry. I'm glad to see it in use and not in that infernal bank vault."

I smiled as brightly as I could considering I was confused as hell and held out my hand. "Henry Warner, ma'am. It's very nice to meet you."

"So, tell me a little bit about yourself, Henry. What is it that you do?"

"I work in a cafe right now, but I'm putting myself through school. It's taking a little longer than I'd like, but I should graduate in the next couple of years."

"And what is it that you are going to school for?"

"I'm getting a business degree."

"Very ambitious. Do you hope to open your own business one day?"

"No, nothing that big. I think I'd lose my mind. I'd rather leave someone else that headache. I just want a good job so I can support myself and my family."

"And will you continue to go to school now that you are engaged to Frank?"

"Of course." I frowned. "Why wouldn't I?"

Eva smiled, but didn't say anything.

"Speaking of school, I really must be going. I have a bunch of studying to do today, but my laptop and everything is back at my place. I was trying to find that Bertram guy so I could leave a message for him to give to Frank. Do you know where he is?"

"I can give Frank a message for you."

"Really? That would be great. I just wanted Frank to know where I was so he didn't worry. I tried to find some paper to leave him a note, but I couldn't so..." I shrugged before holding up my cup. "Thank you again for the coffee. If you tell me where the kitchen is, I can rinse out my cup."

"Maybe you can help an old lady up and then carry that tray into the kitchen for me."

"Of course." I set my cup down on the tray and then stood and stepped over to hold my hands out to the older woman. As soon as she was standing, I picked up the tray. "Just tell me where I'm going."

"Back the way you came."

I cocked my elbow out for her to grab and then we slowly started our way back through the garden to the main corridor. From there, we took a left and headed down the corridor to a swinging door.

Eva pushed it open and then led me inside. The kitchen looked almost how I suspected it would look. Huge, opulent, and expensive. It seemed to be the theme for the entire place.

"Mrs. Rovito," Eva called out. "I'd like to introduce you to Francesco's intended." She smiled up at me. "This is Henry."

I smiled when a rounder older woman glanced at her direction. She had an apron around her waist and a skirt that seemed to go almost to her ankles. Her graying hair was pulled up in a tight bun at the base of her neck.

I nodded respectfully. "Ma'am."

She stared at me for a moment before glancing at Eva. It wasn't until Eva nodded that she smiled at me. I had no idea what had just gone on between them. Apparently, it was a secret language I did not know.

"Where can I put this?" I asked as I raised the tray.

Mrs. Rovito barked out an order and a younger woman dressed in maid's uniform came hurrying over to me to take the tray. "Thank you," I told her.

Her eyebrows rose a bit, but she took the tray without saying a word and hurried away.

I turned and brought Eva's hand to my lips, pressing a kiss to the back of it. "I would very much enjoy having coffee with you again, but I need to get going. I have several hours of studying ahead of me."

Eva patted my cheek. "You go do what you need to do, young man. Never give up on your dreams. Not for anyone or anything."

That was a weird statement to make, but whatever. "Please give my message to Frank."

"I will."

I nodded to Mrs. Rovito. "It was nice meeting you. I'm sure we'll see each other again." If I was going to be living here, I could almost guarantee it.

I could hear the two women start talking in hushed tones as I walked out of the kitchen. It wasn't until I stood outside on the front steps that I realized I had no way to get back into town. I didn't have a car yet—and I wasn't about to wake Frank up to ask him about the car he said he bought me—and I hadn't called a cab.

Well, damn.

"Henry?"

I turned to see Frank's brother stepping out of the house.

"Is everything okay?"

"Yeah, I feel like an idiot. I just forgot to call a cab and I don't have a car."

"What do you need a car for?"

"Oh, I was trying to get back to my apartment. I have a ton of studying to do before class tomorrow."

"I can give you a ride," Martino said. "I'm headed into town now."

I smiled brightly. "That would be great."

It had only been the six of us at dinner last night, Frank's parents, Frank, me, and Martino and his husband. Eva had gone to bed early. Gianni had stayed in town at his dorm at the university.

Martino and I hadn't had much time to talk or get to know each other. His husband seemed to monopolize a majority of his time. It would be nice to have a few minutes to talk to him without being interrupted every time I opened my mouth.

Frankly, I'd been a bit appalled at Stewart's behavior, but I didn't know the man well enough to judge. A number of things could have been going on that I knew nothing about. Besides, any judgment I might have made was still clouded by his insistence that he was supposed to get the ring Frank gave me.

Martino clicked the lock fob in his hand and the lights flashed and alarm beeped on the fancy silver car directly in front of the steps. I'm pretty sure it was a BMW, but I could be wrong. I wasn't that knowledgeable about cars. Might have been why I had not been as excited last night when Frank was telling me about the car he got me.

I waited for Martino to climb into the vehicle before I did. I closed the door and then put on my seatbelt. Martino did the same and then we were underway. We were going a little fast, but I think Martino was just trying to show off for me.

"So, where should I let you off?"

I gave him my address, but said, "Anywhere in town is fine. I can catch a bus."

"No, it's not too far out of my way."

"Thank you."

"So, are you excited about marrying my brother?"

How to answer that?

"I'm excited about marrying Frank Gala. I'm still learning about Francesco Galeazzi."

"He seriously didn't tell you who he was for six months?"

"Nope." I was still fuming over that, but just a little. "I had no idea until yesterday morning when he took me to Mr. Blakely's office and handed me the non-disclosure agreement."

Martino winced. "Yikes."

Yeah, well...

"I hope you won't hold that against him," Martino said. "He means well, but family constraints being what they are..." Martino shrugged. "He didn't really have a choice. We have to be careful that someone isn't with us because of the money we have and not because they care about us." Martino's jaw clenched for just a moment. "Believe me, it's happened before."

From the vehemence in Martino's voice, I had to wonder if he was speaking from personal experience.

"No, I get that, and it's the only reason I'm still wearing Frank's ring, but if he lies to me again, we're going to have serious issues."

"My brother doesn't like to lie, even when the truth is hard. I'm sure he found it as distasteful as you do."

"I hope so." I drew in a heavy breath. "I don't want to marry someone who lies on a regular basis." It would be a marriage that couldn't, and wouldn't, last.

"I heard my mother say something about you attending the university?"

I smiled, glad to be turning the conversation in a different direction. "Yes, I'm going for my business degree."

"How do you like the classes so far?"

I began telling Martino about the courses I'd been taking, which led us to a conversation about the state of corporate owned businesses versus private family owned businesses. Before I knew it, we were pulling up in front of my apartment.

"Are you expecting company?" Martino asked.

"Huh?"

Martino pointed.

I smiled when I saw the sandy haired man sitting on my front step. "Oh, that's Ryan. He's in some of the same business classes as me. We usually end up studying together a lot."

"Does my brother know him?"

"I may have mentioned him, but I'm not sure they've ever really met. I try to get my studying done during the day so my evenings are free to spend with Frank after he gets off work."

I paused as soon as I said that. "I guess that's not going to be a problem anymore. I don't even know what Frank does."

"Our father is chairman of the board of our company. Frank is the CEO."

"That's a lot different than a construction worker."

"Oh man." Martino chuckled. "I would have loved seeing my brother work as a construction worker."

I wiggled my eyebrows. "I have video."

I'd gone by Frank's work site a few times to have lunch with him, and I'd taken my cell phone which had a great camera program. There wasn't a person on the planet that would have disagreed with me taking pictures and videos of that sexy man in his construction gear, working, sweating, and flexing all those muscles.

Yum.

Martino pressed his hands together as if he was praying. "Please, please share and I guarantee you it will win you favorite brother-in-law status."

I laughed as I got out of the car. "Thanks for the ride, Martino." I waved as I dug my keys out of my front pocket and headed for the door of my apartment. "Hey, Ryan." I gave him a quick hug before unlocking my door. "Ready to study?"

Chapter Seven

~ Frank ~

I woke to my cell phone ringing. I reached over to grab it, hoping to turn it off before it woke Henry. "Hello?" I whispered.

"Hey, Frank, it's Martino."

"What do you want?" Didn't he realize how early it was?

"I dropped Henry off at his apartment and he—"

"Wait, you what?" I glanced to the other side of the mattress, but it was empty. I was the only one in the room. I sat up and then rubbed my hand over my face. "Okay, one more time."

"I dropped Henry off at his apartment. He said he needed to study."

Even though I wished Henry had woken me before leaving, I understood. "Yeah, he has exams coming up next week."

"Some guy was waiting for him. Henry said his name was Ryan?"

I'd heard of Ryan before, of course. "They're study buddies."

"Is business all they are studying? Because they looked pretty friendly. Henry even gave him a hug."

"That's just Henry. He hugs all of his friends." It had taken me awhile to get used to that, but eventually I'd figured out that Henry was a friendly person, especially to those he cared about.

"Okay, I just wanted to check."

I knew why Martino was worried. Before he met Stewart, he'd become involved with someone who had put him through the ringer. He'd only been with Martino because of the money and had even started sleeping around behind Martino's back.

The man had been a gold digger right down to his little black soul, and the basis for every precaution my family now took. We were all cautious now.

I smiled even though Martino couldn't see it. "It's fine, Martino. I promise."

"Okay."

I hung up my phone and tossed it onto the bed in front of me. I was thankful that my brother was looking out for me, but I was sure of Henry. I wouldn't have asked him to marry me if I wasn't.

Speaking of Henry... I picked up my phone again and dialed Henry's number.

"Hello?"

"Morning, baby."

"Frank." I could hear the happiness in his voice. "When did you wake up?"

"Apparently, not early enough to see my fiancé leave."

"Sorry about that. You looked like you needed your sleep. I did leave a message with your grandmother when we had coffee this morning. I couldn't find a piece of paper to leave you a note."

My eyebrows lifted in surprise. "You had coffee with my grandmother?"

"Yes, and she's wonderful. I even got to meet Mrs. Rovito."

My eyebrows lifted a little bit more. "You were allowed in the kitchen?"

"Was I not supposed to be?"

"We're never allowed in the kitchen."

"Oh, well, I had to drop off the tray so your grandmother wouldn't have to carry it. I guess I should apologize to Mrs. Rovito."

"No, no." I chuckled. "If she didn't chase you out with one of her wooden spoons, you're good."

"A wooden spoon?"

"Oh yes." I shuddered. I'd been on the receiving end of that wooden spoon more than once. "How's studying going?"

"Slowly," Henry groaned. "Neither Ryan or I get this acquisitions thing one of our professors was talking about. We've been going over our notes and what we've read in the text book, but it just doesn't make sense."

"I might know a thing or two about that. Why don't I get in the fancy new metallic blue BMW convertible sitting in the garage and come help you out?"

Henry snickered. "Oh, so you get to drive my new car before me?"

"I already drove your new car. How do you think it got to the garage?"

"Hey, could you bring food? I'm starving and my kitchen is a little bare."

"I can probably do that."

"Are you going to stay here tonight or go back to your place?"

I frowned. "You don't want to come back to the house?"

"I have school tomorrow, Frank."

"You also have a car now, Henry."

"Oh, right. Huh."

I chuckled. "Pack a bag and you can drive your car back here after we study so that you are used to it and can take it to school tomorrow."

"I'll have to leave early. I'll need to stop by the school and get a parking pass."

"Already done, babe."

"You got me a parking pass?"

"Of course, I did. You're a student. You have to have one to park in the student parking lot."

"That's why I'm marrying you Frank, not because you bought me a fancy blue car."

I smiled. "I know, and that's why I'm marrying you, because you care more about me getting you a parking pass than a fancy blue car."

"See you soon, yeah?"

"Yeah, I need to jump in the shower and grab some food and then I'll be on my way."

"Okay, see you when you get here."

I still had a smile on my face when I hung up. Henry was proving to me over and over again why he was the right choice. My money really meant nothing to him. My thinking about him and putting him first did.

I tossed my phone on the bed and then went to go take a shower. I might have been a little quicker than I should have been, but I wanted to get to Henry's apartment. When I walked out of the bathroom, I was thankful I had a towel wrapped around my waist.

"What are you doing?"

Stewart jumped dropping my phone back onto the bed. "Oh, nothing. I came to see if you and Henry wanted to have lunch, but I couldn't find you and then your phone started ringing."

"Henry already left for his place and I'm joining him there for lunch," I said as I walked over to the bed to pick up my phone. "Maybe another time."

I was not thrilled that the man was in my bedroom. I didn't like him in my suite, but the bedroom was worse. This was my private space. No one should be in here except Henry. I didn't even let the maid come in here to clean. I did that myself.

"You need to go, Stewart."

Stewart smiled and sauntered toward me, looking me up and down before he licked his lips. I stepped back when he tried to stroke his finger down my chest. "I could stay."

I immediately lifted my phone and dialed Martino. "Tell your husband to get out of my bedroom before I have him arrested for sexual assault."

I hung up and pointed toward the door. I knew what kind of man Stewart was, and this just proved it. I wasn't going to be put in a position where Stewart could make me seem as if I was being unfaithful to Henry, and it had nothing to do with the ten million dollars stated in the pre-nup. I simply wouldn't hurt Henry like that.

Stewart gasped as turned pale white before his face flushed red when his phone started ringing. He pulled out his phone and answered it. "What?" he shouted as he stormed toward the door. "You're being ridiculous. I would never do that."

I shook my head as Stewart's voice faded, but didn't move from my spot until I heard the door to my suite open and then slam shut. I wish there was something I could do to get Martino out of that marriage. It had been fucked up since before they said their vows.

Unfortunately, the only one who could do something about it was Martino, and he didn't seem to be there yet. I suspected he was trying to save his marriage and that maybe he did care about Stewart on some level. I just wished Stewart cared about him.

I walked over to my dresser and pulled out clean underwear, a T-shirt, socks, and a pair of jeans. I'd gotten used to wearing jeans while I'd been on my hiatus. I didn't relish the idea of going back to suits, but I knew I'd need to once I went back to work at the company.

Today, I was going to study with Henry, so I could get away with jeans.

I stuck my phone in my pocket, made sure I had my wallet, keys, and sunglasses, and then headed out of the bedroom. I made a quick stop in my study to grab the file I'd started for Henry. It had the deed for his cottage and the registration and ownership paperwork for his car.

I needed the car paperwork, and I was pretty sure the deed would help me explain acquisitions to him. It's how my father explained it to me, although it had been a bicycle and not a cottage, but the idea was the same.

Once I had everything, I grabbed my jacket and headed downstairs. I could hear crying coming from Martino and Stewart's suite as I passed it. I felt a little bad for the guy, but not enough to stop and offer comfort. Who knew how he'd take that?

"Bertram, good," I said when I spotted the guy just as I reached the bottom of the stairs. "Could you ask Mrs. Rovito if she could make up some sandwiches for three? I'm driving into town to help Henry and his study partner out with some stuff for one of their classes and none of us have eaten."

"Of course, sir."

After Bertram walked away, I headed down the hallway to my father's office. I'd never known him not to be in his office by eight o'clock in the morning unless it was the weekend or a holiday. And he might be semi-retired, but he still worked almost as hard as me and Martino did.

I knocked on the door when I reached it because I had learned my lesson about barging into rooms when I was a kid and those were memories I wished I could bleach out of my mind. Needless to say, my parents had a very healthy marriage.

"Come."

I opened the door and walked in. I took a seat in the chair in front of my father's desk. "Good morning, Papa."

"Good morning, son." Bellino glanced behind me. "No fiancé?"

"Henry left with Martino this morning so he could start studying. He has exams next week and needs all the study time he can get."

"Ah." My father smiled. "So, when can I expect you back at work?"

"I'd like to give it another week. I want to get Henry moved in here first, but that might take a little convincing." I held up the manila envelope in my hand. "I'm taking his car to him today to sweeten the deal."

"You need to buy him a car to sweeten the deal?"

"No, and he's actually a little upset with me that I did buy him a car, but he needs a way to get to and from school and his job. Taking a taxi everyday is too damn expensive."

"I could see that."

"Henry tried to talk me into something cheaper, but this car has a really good safety rating and I think he'll really like it once he drives it."

"I'm beginning to suspect that you cannot buy your fiancé."

"Nope." I chuckled. "He was more excited that I took the time to get him a student parking pass than he was that I got him a car."

"Sounds like a good man."

I leaned forward, resting my elbows on my knees. "How do you deal with that? I mean, you and Mama raised us to appreciate money, but to know it is not what binds people together. Henry never had anything he didn't work his fingers to the bone for. How do I spoil him and give him the world when he gets mad at me for buying him gifts?"

"You do it carefully," Bellino replied. "Your mother is much the same way. Yes, she lives in a fancy house with a butler, a cook, and a couple of maids, but that is all window dressing, things we needed to keep the status quo when our business became so profitable. These are not the things that make your mother happy."

"So, what do you suggest?"

"Take him flowers, go for a drive, have lunch with him, and spend time with him. That is the most precious commodity you have. Your time. Make sure you always have time for him."

Maybe I was doing this right. "I'm waiting for Mrs. Rovito to make us some sandwiches and then I'm driving into town to help Henry and his study partner with some of their school work that they are having issues with."

"That's a good start."

I smiled. I could do this.

"Was that what you wanted to see me about, son?"

"No." My happiness fled. "This needs to stay between us, although Martino knows because I called him. When I came out of the shower, I found Stewart in my bedroom looking through my phone. I told him to leave and he made a pass at me. I immediately called Martino and told him to tell Stewart to get out, but you know how Stewart is. I don't want any of this falling back on Henry."

Bellino's lips twisted into a grimace. "I do not know why that idiot brother of yours doesn't cut Stewart loose. That man is no good for him. Martino is miserable, and it gets worse if he denies Stewart whatever new shiny bauble he wants."

"He wants Grandfather's ring." I had no doubt he was going to try and find a way to get it, too. Just because it was mine and I had given it to Henry did not mean Stewart had given up on getting it. It might not be as shiny as the other jewelry Martino had given him, but he wanted it, probably even more so now that Henry had it.

"I will speak with your brother tonight when he gets home from work."

"I'm sorry you're getting dragged into this, Papa. I have a really bad feeling about this, especially after what he did in my bedroom."

"What exactly did he do?"

I quickly explained to my father exactly what had gone on since the moment I walked out of the bathroom until the door slammed shut behind Stewart. I even added the part about hearing Stewart crying when I was coming downstairs.

"All right, son, you go spend the afternoon with Henry. I'll take care of your brother and his husband."

"Thank you, Papa." I got up and hurried out of the room.

I so didn't want to be around for that conversation.

Chapter Eight

~ Frank ~

I signed the last contract I needed to sign and then closed the folder my secretary had given me. It was after hours and I'd been working late tonight to try and get some extra work done so I could spend tomorrow with Henry. Besides, he was studying with Ryan and wasn't expected home until around ten or so.

Home, that had taken on a whole new meaning over the last month. For one—and by far the most important thing—Henry was now living with me. Technically, he hadn't officially moved in, but more and more of his stuff was appearing in our suite every day and he spent every night in my arms. I was hoping to convince him to move in the last of his stuff as soon as the semester was over and his lease ran out.

I glanced up when my door slammed open and then shot to my feet. "What is he doing here?" I asked my brother.

Stewart had been kicked out a few days after propositioning me in my bedroom. As far as I knew, Martino had filed for divorce and hadn't seen him since, so I had no idea why they were together now.

Martino held up his hand. "Just listen."

My nostrils flared with anger as I glanced at Stewart.

Stewart eyes me like a lion to a lamb. "I have evidence that your precious little fiancé isn't as sweet and innocent as you'd like to believe."

"Bullshit!" I snapped.

"No, he's right, Frank," Martino said before glancing at his soon-to-be ex-husband. "Show him the texts you showed me."

I frowned when Stewart pulled out a cell phone with a rainbow cover. I instantly recognized the colorful cover. "Why do you have Henry's cell phone?" I'd bought Henry a new one when he lost his about a week ago. I guess now I knew what had happened to it.

"Just look." Stewart handed me Henry's phone. The message app was open.

My heart started to sink as I began reading through Henrys messages. I knew Henry wouldn't be unfaithful to me, but it would be hard to explain these texts.

Ryan: I got it.

Henry: Seriously?

Ryan: Yep, I'm holding it in my hot little hand.

Henry: Oh man, I love you so much right now.

* * * *

Henry: Can you come over? Frank just left. We have the whole night.

Ryan: I'll be right over.

Henry: Don't forget your clothes.

* * * *

Ryan: Does he suspect anything?

Henry: No.

Ryan: When are you going to tell him?

Henry: I'm afraid to tell him.

Ryan: You need to tell him.

* * * *

Ryan: Either tell him or I will.

Henry: He's going to be so mad.

Ryan: Probably, but you have to tell him.

Henry: I will, I promise.

Ryan: Soon, Henry, or I will.

Henry: I said I'd tell him and I will.

I tossed Henry's phone on the desk. "This doesn't mean anything."

"Frank!" Martino shouted. "He's fucking around on you with that study buddy of his."

"No, he's not," I said vehemently, although I wasn't positive of it anymore. Those texts were pretty damning.

"I have more proof," Stewart said, "but it's going to cost you."

"You're lying and trying to get money out of me because you got booted out on your ass for making a pass at me."

"I might be mad at you, but I'm not lying. Of course, I didn't expect you to believe me so I have a sample of my evidence." Stewart pulled a picture out of his jacket pocket and tossed it down onto the desk. "If you want the rest of them, it's going to cost you."

I was surprised I kept my hand from shaking as I reached for the picture. Once I looked at it, I wanted to scream and rage. I wanted to wrap my fingers around Henry's lying little neck and squeeze and then I wanted to rip his heart out like he was doing to me.

There was no mistaking the way Ryan was holding Henry as anything other than a lover's embrace. He looked as if he was getting ready to kiss Henry. Neither man had their shirts on, leaving me with no doubt what they were about to do.

I looked up. "How much?"

"Five million dollars."

I knew my voice was cold and lifeless by the crinkle in Martino's brow. I just couldn't help it. I felt dead inside. "Will a wire transfer do?"

"Yes." Stewart held out a piece of paper with his account number on it.

I sat down at my desk and opened my banking page so I could type in the information needed to transfer the money to Stewart's account.

"Frank," Martino said, "maybe you should talk to Henry before you do this. There could be a plausible explanation."

"If you expect to reach Henry right now, you should know he's not studying, but he is with Ryan. I went by his apartment on my way here and they were just leaving."

I ignored my brother and Stewart, kept typing, and then hit enter. "There it's done. Now give me the evidence."

Stewart glanced down at his phone, tapped a couple of buttons, and then smiled before reaching into his jacket to pull out a small manila envelope. I took it and opened it, dumping the contents out on the desk.

More pictures.

I glanced up at Stewart. "Get out, and if I see you here again, I'll have you arrested for trespassing."

Stewart smirked. "I got what I wanted."

He turned and walked out of the room, the door shutting behind him.

I picked up the first picture in the stack. It was another picture of Ryan holding Henry, only this time, Henry was laughing. There were shots of him stretched out on the sofa at his apartment, his head in Ryan's lap, shots of them eating together, and one where Ryan's head was resting against Henry's.

So many pictures and each one more damning than the last one.

The one that killed any hope that this was all wrong was the one of the two of them in Henry's bed together, both naked. Henry was sitting behind Ryan with his arms wrapped around him, one hand on Ryan's chest. I could see my grandfather's ring bright as day on the hand Henry had wrapped around Ryan's dick.

"What are you going to do?" Martino asked.

"What I am not going to do is marry that fucking little gold digger."

"You don't know that he was after your money, Frank. This might not even have anything to do with money. Maybe...maybe they just sort of fell in love or something."

Oh, that was so much better.

"Fine, then they can be in love somewhere else." I stuffed all the pictures and Henry's phone into the envelope and then reached for my suit coat. I tucked the envelope into the pocket before pulling it on.

"Frank, look, I know this looks damning, but maybe you should talk to Henry before you do something rash. You're hurt right now and not thinking with a clear head."

"My head is perfectly clear," I said as my anger became a scalding fury.

I knew exactly what I needed to do.

* * * *

~ Henry ~

"It's going to be fine, Henry."

I wasn't so sure of that. "We never discussed this, Ryan. Frank is going to flip."

I knew I was and I'd had a couple of hours to grow used to the idea.

"Just tell him, Henry. I'll bet you'll be surprised by his reaction."

Oh, I had no doubt, but I was still convinced that Frank was going to flip. Neither of us had planned on this. Not really.

"You never know what's going to happen until you talk to Frank. When you get home, take him upstairs to your bedroom, sit him on the bed, and tell him."

"Yeah." I knew I had no other choice. "I'll call you tomorrow to tell you how it went."

"Call me tonight if you need me."

"Thanks." I was really hoping that I wouldn't. "I need to go. I'm almost home."

"Talk to you tomorrow."

I clicked the button on the steering wheel to disconnect my phone. That was one of many features my new car had. I was still trying to learn them all. I was pretty sure it was going to take me awhile. This thing practically cooked me dinner.

When I reached the family estate, I pulled up in front of the gates and hit the unlock button. When they slowly swung open, Frank's father was standing there. I frowned at the glower on the man's face before turning off the engine and climbing out of the vehicle.

"Papa, is everything okay?" I didn't understand the rigid set of the man's jaw as he walked toward me and held out an envelope. "What's going on?" I glanced toward the house. "Where's Frank?"

"You will never see my son again."

My head snapped around as I gasped. "What are you talking about?"

"We know what you did, Henry, and I am very disappointed in you. I thought you truly loved my son, but you had us all fooled, didn't you? I must say, you are a very good actor. You might want to consider that as a career instead of business."

I admit I was hurt by Bellino's words, but I was more concerned with what the man was accusing me of. "What do you think that I did?"

"I know what you did, Henry. I've seen the evidence with my very own eyes."

Ryan was right. I should have told Frank that I had dented my brand new car. "Okay, so I didn't tell Frank about the dent, but that is no reason to—"

"You think this is about some little dent?" Bellino barked at me.

I took a quick step back, afraid of the man for the very first time. "Papa—"

"You no longer have the right to call me by that name. You may address me as Mr. Galeazzi."

I swallowed past the bile rising in my throat and tried again. "If that's what you want, Mr. Galeazzi. I—"

"What I want is for you to go away and never come back. What I want is for my son to forget he ever met you. What I want...What I want is for you to suffer the same pain and anguish you are putting Francesco through."

Tears flooded my eyes when I realized this was no joke, and it wasn't about the dent in the car. I still didn't understand what was going on, though. "Mr. Galeazzi, please, if you would just let me talk to Frank—"

"Like I said, you will never speak to my son again."

"I need to speak to him."

"It's not going to happen. I've already removed your access to the estate. If you step one foot on it, you will be arrested for trespassing."

"But—"

Bellino snapped his fingers. Bertram walked forward with two duffle bags. He set them on the ground at my feet and then turned and walked back inside the estate grounds.

"I took the liberty of having all of your belongings packed for you," Bellino said before waving the envelope at me. "This is five thousand dollars. It should be enough to get you set up somewhere."

I smacked the envelope away. "I don't want your money." My voice was high and shrill, desperate. "I want to talk to Frank!"

I shivered a little at Bellino's expression of anger and hatred. "Go now," the man snapped, "go before I am forced to call the police."

"Let me talk to Frank!"

Bellino ignored me. He picked up the envelope and tucked it into one of my bags before turning and walking back through the open gate. I started to run after him, but four very large, very armed men stepped between us.

Tears rolled down my cheeks as the gates closed with a heavy and ominous clank. I couldn't believe this was happening. I still didn't know what I was supposed to have done. No one would tell me, which meant I had no way to defend myself.

I walked back to my car and climbed inside. I swallowed the despair in my throat and picked up my phone. I dialed Frank's number, but the phone message said I had been blocked. I tried messaging him. It wouldn't send. I called the main house, but my number had been blocked there, too.

I didn't know who else to call so I just sat there. I'd sit there until morning when someone came out— hopefully Frank—and I could get inside. I'd be damned if I gave up without a fight.

More tears flooded my eyes and slid down my cheeks as I covered my abdomen with my hand. I wasn't the only one I was fighting for.

Chapter Nine

~ Henry ~

I jerked awake when someone knocked on the car window. For a brief, heart pounding moment, I thought it was Frank. I eagerly rolled the window down until I realized I was face to face with a police officer.

"Can I help you, officer?"

I was afraid I already knew what he was going to say.

"Sir, I'm afraid I'm going to have to ask you to leave the premises or I'll have to arrest you for trespassing."

Yep, I knew it.

"Thank you, officer." I shot a quick look toward the mansion. The four guards were still standing there. "I'll leave."

"Are these your bags, sir?"

I glanced down at the two bags another officer was holding in his hands. "I'm not sure."

I climbed out of the car, took the bags, and set them on the hood. I quickly unzipped the bags and started going through them. I guess they were mine. Everything inside certainly was. I doubted a single item of mine was left inside the mansion.

I grabbed the envelope Bellino had put in there last night and held it out to the officer. "You can give this back to Mr. Bellino. It doesn't belong to me."

"I'll see that he gets it," the officer said as he took the envelope.

I tossed the bags into the back of my car and then climbed behind the wheel. I made sure I had my seatbelt on before I started the car and backed out onto the road and then started driving back toward the city.

I knew I still needed to talk to Frank, even if it was just to tell him about the baby, but my misery was starting to turn to anger. I didn't know what I was supposed to have done, and I was starting to not care. If they could find me guilty without giving me a chance to defend myself, then they weren't the people I thought they were.

They certainly weren't people I wanted my child raised around.

I still had to tell Frank, though. It was the right thing to do. This was his child as much as it was mine. He had a right to know he was going to be a father. I just had to figure out a way to talk to him without his family around or the guards or the police.

I didn't see a lot of options.

I called Ryan and asked him to meet me at my apartment. Hopefully, he would be able to give me some ideas because I was all out. Or maybe it was because I couldn't stop thinking about the hateful words Bellino had shouted out at me or that Frank believed whatever nonsense was going on.

I guess he didn't trust me as much as he said he did.

I was thankful when my apartment came into view because I was a blubbering mess. I was pretty sure the tear steaks going down my face were going to engrave themselves into my cheekbones.

I parked my car, grabbed my bags, and then walked into my apartment. I dropped the bags right inside the door and walked inside. I made it as far as the couch before I collapsed and started crying.

That's where Ryan found me. I felt his arms wrap around me and just turned and buried my face in his neck.

"Hey, hey, it can't be that bad, whatever it is."

"Frank's father met me at the gate to the estate when I got home. He had my bags all packed. He handed me an envelope full of money before telling me I would never see Frank again and that he wanted me to go away."

"What?" Ryan leaned back so he could see my face. "Why?"

"I don't know. No one will tell me. I don't know what I did."

"Did you try calling him?"

I nodded. "My number was blocked."

"I could try."

I nodded again as I sat up. "Would you?"

Ryan pulled out his cell phone. He already had Frank's number in case he couldn't get a hold of me. He dialed, but after a moment he lowered his phone and shook his head. "My number has been blocked, too."

"I don't understand what is going on. What did I do that was so bad?"

"Did you ask him for money?"

"No, I've never asked Frank or any of his family for money. I've always tried to make it real clear to all of them that I wasn't with Frank because he had money."

"Did you fool around on him?"

"No, I would never."

Ryan winced. "You don't think this is about the dent, do you?"

"No, I started to tell Mr. Galeazzi about the dent, but he said he didn't care."

"Mr. Galeazzi?"

The tears started to flow again. "Frank's father."

"I thought he told you to call him Papa."

"He changed his mind. He said I can only call him Mr. Galeazzi now."

"Bastard!"

My heart leapt into his throat when someone knocked on the front door. "It's Frank. It has to be." I jumped up and started for the door.

Ryan caught me by the arm. "You go wash your face. I'll answer the door."

That was probably a good idea.

I raced into my bedroom to the bathroom and turned on the cold water before glancing at myself in the mirror. Yeah, it was a real good idea. I looked like crap.

I splashed some water on my face and then dried it with a clean hand towel. Before I left the bathroom, I ran a brush through my hair. I tried to put a smile on my face as I walked out of the bathroom, but the sour look on Ryan's face instantly erased it.

Ryan's jaw clenched before he said, "It's not Frank."

I swallowed tightly. "Who...Who is it?"

"His brother Martino."

I drew in a calming breath before pushing past Ryan and walking out into the living room. Maybe Martino could tell me what in the hell is going on. "Martino."

The man turned from the window he was staring out of. "Why am I not surprised to find you two together?"

What?

"Where's Frank? I need to speak to him."

"Frank doesn't want to speak to you. In fact, he never wants to see you again." Martino pulled two envelopes out of his pocket. "This is a check for one million dollars. Frank felt it was only right for you to have it. Personally, I think it's a little much to pay for a well-used whore, but it's his money."

I couldn't even gasp. I felt as if someone had just driven a dagger into my heart. I wasn't even sure it was still beating anymore.

"Get out, you son-of-a-bitch!" Ryan shouted.

"Oh, I'm going," Martino said with a smirk on his face. "I just have one more thing to give you. This is a restraining order barring you from being within five hundred feet of any Galeazzi, our places of residence, or our businesses. If you do attempt to see us or are found on any of these properties, you will be arrested and thrown in jail for what I hope is a very, very long time."

With that, Martino walked out, slamming the door behind him.

It sounded like a death knell.

I know I was numb because all I could do was stand there and stare at the two envelopes on the table. I didn't want to touch either of them. I knew my life would end if I did.

"Henry." Ryan's voice was soft and gentle, but I barely heard him. "Henry, come on, man. Snap out of it."

A bitter cold of despair dwelt within the deepest reaches of my soul. I closed my eyes, my heart aching with the pain. How was I supposed to survive this?

I have no idea how much time had passed before Ryan's voice tunneled through my misery and started to make sense. "Hey, Henry, you need to listen to me. You've had enough time to wallow in your misery. It's time for you to wake up and start making some decisions."

I opened my eyes and realized that it was light outside. "Wha—" I had to swallow hard before I could speak again. "What time is it?"

"About ten o'clock in the morning."

"Wow." I rubbed my hands over my face. "I guess I was out of it there for a little while, huh?"

"It's Thursday, Henry. You've been out of it for two days."

My eyes rounded. "Shit."

That would explain the smell.

"Why don't you go jump in the shower while I make you some breakfast and then we can sit down and talk?"

I nodded absently. "I didn't imagine that Frank kicked me to the curb, right?"

"No." Ryan snorted. "He more than kicked you to the curb, he erased your ass."

Yeah, that's what I thought.

I refused to let anymore tears fall as I got up and walked to the bathroom. I peeled my clothes off and dropped them in the hamper before climbing into the shower. I felt icy fingers in every pore of my body, freezing me from the inside out. Nothing really felt real.

The shower made me feel at least human, if nothing else. After drying off, I pulled on a clean set of clothes and then walked out into the main room. Ryan was sitting at the dining room table drinking a cup of coffee.

"I wasn't sure how your stomach was, so I made you some oatmeal."

"Thank you."

Ryan was kind of enough to let me eat in peace. He didn't start talking until after I had finished, taken my bowl into the kitchen to rinse out, and then sat back down.

And then he hit me with both barrels by slapping the two envelopes down on the table in front of me. "It's time for you to make some decisions."

"I'm not sure I can."

"You don't have much choice, Henry. It's not just you that you have to think about. Frank or not, you are bringing a child into the world." Ryan cocked an eyebrow. "Unless you don't want to, but that decision has to be made soon, too."

I instantly covered my abdomen with both hands as if protect the life growing inside of me. "I'm not getting rid of my baby."

"I didn't think you would, but that means you have some hard decisions to make."

"You keep mentioning decisions. What decisions?"

"Where you're going to live? How you're going to support yourself and a kid? Are you going to continue to go to school?" Ryan grabbed one of the envelopes and shook it. "Are you going to take this guilt money to make your life easier or shove it back in his face?" Ryan shrugged. "Those kind of decisions."

That was a lot.

"I won't take a penny from Francesco Galeazzi or his family."

"Okay, then you'll have to support yourself."

My heart sank a little more as I realized my priorities in life had shifted. "And drop out of school. I can't afford to pay rent, go to school, and raise a kid." The cafe didn't pay that well.

"Well, we can move in together. That should cut down on some of your bills."

My eyebrows lifted. "You want to live with me and my kid?"

"Actually." Ryan leaned back in his chair and rubbed his abdomen. "I was thinking you and your kid could live with me and my kid."

My jaw dropped.

"I kind of met this guy and had a one night stand with him. After we did the nasty, he told me he was married and wanted nothing to do with me, so I guess I'm on my own."

A burst of laughter left my lips. "Oh, we are a pair, aren't we?"

"I have a few suggestions if you want to listen."

I nodded. Anything would be better than what I had, which was nothing. "Go ahead."

"How do you feel about Seattle, Washington?"

Chapter Ten

~ Frank ~

"Is that everything?" Frank knew he was a little brisk, but that seemed to be the way of things lately.

"Yes, sir."

My secretary made her exit as quickly as she could. I didn't really blame her. I'd been short with everyone over the last two weeks. I was angry, enraged, and livid. Take any one of those descriptive words and they all meant the same thing. I was pissed.

I was also hurt. I had given my heart to Henry and he'd kicked me to the ground, and for what? More money? Once we were married, I would have given him the world.

He should have stuck it out like Stewart did. He'd walked away from his marriage to Martino with a cool five million dollars, and then gotten another five million from me. He should be living on easy street.

I spent the first few days after kicking Henry out drowning my sorrows in the biggest bottle of booze that I could find. After my mother had dragged me out of it, I swore I was going to devote myself to my work and nothing else. So, here I was at work, except it wasn't working. I still thought about Henry constantly.

The door opened and my father walked in, followed closely by Martino. I turned to face the two men. "Papa, Martino, to what do I owe this visit?"

As if I didn't already know.

"We need to talk, Francesco," Papa said.

"No, we really don't."

"I think you should take some time and get your head together," my father continued as if I hadn't said anything. "This has been a very trying time for all of us, and you need to take some time for yourself."

I rolled my eyes as I said, "No, I don't."

"You do, brother," Martino said. "You practically took Marianne's head off the other day when she didn't get your coffee order right."

"Several of the staff have mentioned how angry you seem to be, son. And while I understand your anger, it needs to be directed at the person who made you angry, not our innocent staff members."

My shoulders slumped. "Maybe you're right. Maybe I do need to take a little time off."

I just didn't want to because every time I was alone with my thoughts, they turned to Henry. I had this big aching hole in the middle of my chest where he used to be.

I wanted him back.

I was starting to think maybe I should have talked to him instead of letting my family handle it. Maybe we could have gone to counseling or something. I know I was grasping at ideas, but I never thought I'd miss him so damn much.

"Come," I said when someone knocked on my office door. The door opened and my secretary stood there. "What is it, Marianne?"

"There's a delivery for you, sir, but you have to sign for it."

I frowned, but waved my hand at her. "Send the delivery person in."

Marianne stood back and a man in stepped in wearing a well know courier service uniform. "Mr. Galeazzi?"

"Could you be more specific, son?" my father asked. "There are three Galeazzis sitting here."

"Oh." The man glanced down at the front a thin, rectangular box he held in his hand. "Mr. Francesco Galeazzi."

I raised my hand. "That would be me."

"Um, I'm supposed to ask for ID, sir."

I glanced at my brother and father before standing and pulling my wallet out of my pocket. I grabbed my license and handed it over. The guy looked it over before handing it back and then handed me a piece of paper.

"Can you sign here, sir? It's acknowledging that you received the package."

Normally, I wouldn't sign it until I knew exactly what I was receiving and then knowing it was all there, but this was a very reputable firm, and one I used often. I signed and then took the package.

"Have a good day, sir," the man said before walking out of the room.

Marianne closed the door as she walked out.

"Were you expecting a package, son?"

I shook my head as I turned it over until I could see the label. "It's from Blakely's office."

I tore the end off of the package and then dumped the contents out on my desk. There were two smaller boxes inside along with a legal file. An envelope with my name on it was taped to the front of the file.

I grabbed the envelope and opened it, then took the paper inside out and started reading it. About half way through, I forgot how to breathe.

Dear, Mr. Galeazzi,

As it would violate the terms of the restraining order issued against my client for him to contact you directly, Mr. Henry Warner has retained my services to return these items to you. He wishes for me to assure you that he will adhere to the letter of the law concerning the restraining order you have filed against him. After this, he will in no way try to contact you, any member of your family, or set foot onto any property belonging to the Galeazzi family.

Contained with this letter you will find:

1. *The deed to the cottage given to Mr. Warner during your time together. It has been deeded back to you and the appropriate papers filed with the county clerk's office.*
2. *The title to one metallic blue 2021 BMW 8 Series 840i Convertible. The keys are inside and the*

car can be found in the parking lot a block from
your place of business.

3. *A check made out to him for one million dollars.*
4. *One antique men's ring once belonging to Arturo*
   Galeazzi.

If you have any questions concerning the items I have
listed, please give me a call at 555-2323.
Sincerely, Edward Blakely, Esq.

"Son, what is it? You've gone past white."

"It's...uh...it's a letter from Blakely. It seems that Henry hired him to deliver this stuff to me." I frowned as I scanned the letter one more time. "Who filed a restraining order against him?"

I hadn't.

"I did," Martino said. "I didn't want him coming around trying to convince you to go back to him or trying to get more money out of you." Martino swallowed hard before saying, "I didn't expect him to give the money back."

"Why not?" my father asked. "He gave back the money I tried to give him when I met him at the gate."

"He's given back the cottage, the car, the money." I picked up the two boxes and opened them. One had a set of keys in it. The other box held my grandfather's ring. I held it between my fingers and stared at it. "And my grandfather's ring."

"He gave everything back?" Martino asked.

I drew in a heavy breath. "Everything except the ring I gave him when I proposed." Why did it hurt so much to know the one thing he had kept was the cheapest item of all? "I think that maybe Henry and I need to talk."

"Do you think that's wise, son?"

"Probably not, but I think we need closure if nothing else."

"You blocked his number," Martino said. "How are you going to get a hold of him?"

"I'll go by his apartment."

"What about the restraining order? If you seek him out, it negates it."

"I never wanted a restraining order, Martino. I don't know why you had one issued. Henry is not some mad stalker."

Martino snorted. "That you know of, but you didn't think he'd be unfaithful to you either."

I couldn't argue with that.

"I still think Henry and I need to talk, even if it's just to resolve all of this." I put all the paperwork—minus the million dollar check—back into the box along with the keys to the car. I was keeping the ring with me. I slid it onto my finger. My grandfather wanted me to have it, so I'd wear it from now on.

I stood and grabbed my suit jacket. "I'm going to be out for the rest of the day."

"Be careful, son."

"I will be." I left my father and brother sitting in my office as I walked out. "Marianne, I'm going to be out the rest of the afternoon. Please reschedule any appointments I had today."

"Yes, sir."

I stopped before I'd taken more than a couple of steps and turned to face my secretary of five years. "Marianne, I need to apologize for my behavior the last two weeks. The breakup with my fiancé is hitting me a little harder than I expected. That's still not an excuse, but an explanation."

"I understand, sir."

"The next time I step out of line, tell my father. He'll kick me back into play."

A small smile graced Marianne's lips. "I'll do that, sir."

I started to think as I continued walking toward the elevator. After everything that had occurred, I had no idea how I was going to get Henry to talk to me. I wasn't about to beg, but I really felt we needed to discuss the situation.

I was adamant that Henry take the money. As angry as I was, I still cared about him. I knew how important his education was to him. With that money, he could attend any university in the country without having to have a job to support himself.

After getting downstairs to my car and getting out on the road, it took almost an hour to get to the other side of town. Traffic was one of the things I truly hated about living in the city. By the time I pulled up in front of Henry's apartment, I was ready to ram the next asshole driver with my car.

I parked in front of his apartment and got out. I noticed the for 'rent sign' in the window as I was going up the stairs. I felt a scream of frustration at the back of my throat. I hurried up the rest of the steps and then stood on the edge of the porch so I could lean over and look into the window.

A lot of furniture was still inside, but no personal items. The place was practically bare. I glanced at the 'for rent' sign, found the number at the bottom, and the called. "Hello, I'm looking for Henry Warner. I came by his apartment, but it's empty."

"Sorry, man, Henry moved."

"When?"

"I don't know, a week ago? The place has been cleaned though, so if you're interested—"

"Where did he move to?" I asked.

"How the hell would I know?"

"What about his mail? How are you supposed to forward his mail?"

"He put a stop on it at the post office."

Fuck!

"Are you sure you're not interested in the apartment. It's a one bedroom—"

I hung up and then dialed Henry's phone number. Disconnected.

I tried Ryan's phone number, figuring he would know where Henry was. They were sleeping together after all, but it was disconnected as well.

I ran back down the steps and climbed into my car. I drove by his work first, but they told me he had quit last week, no notice. The school wouldn't tell me where he was or what classes he had until I showed them the check and told them that it was meant for his tuition and I was trying to find him to give it to him. They simply told me he had dropped out of school.

I slowly made my way back out to my car and then sat inside, staring through the windshield at nothing. There would be no closure for me. No closure for Henry. No finding out if what we had together was salvageable.

Henry Warner had disappeared.

Chapter Eleven

~ Henry ~

5 Years Later...

I smiled at the receptionist as she let me into the large conference room. I was a little bit early, but I wanted to make sure I was all set up before the client came in. I made my way to one of the chairs near the front of the table, but on the side. I'd learned early on in my career to never sit at the end of the table. That was always reserved for the client.

After sitting down, I opened my briefcase and pulled out my laptop. I turned it on. While waiting for it to boot up, I pulled out a legal pad and a pencil. Something else I had also learned was not to use a pen until the final version of the project was decided on.

"Oh, Mr. Warner, good, you're here."

I smiled as I stood and held out my hand. "Good morning, Mr. Simpson."

The man shook my hand. "The new owner just arrived. He'll be here in a few minutes."

"Okay."

"Did you get the file I sent you?"

"I did and I've updated my calculations. I've brought a printout if you can get someone to make some copies." I reached into my briefcase and pulled out the file I'd compiled. I handed it over. "Everything is in here. I can, of course, explain it as we go through it."

Mr. Simpson started leafing through the pages of the file I had given him. "This is amazing work, Mr. Warner."

I didn't say anything. I knew it was good work because I had put my blood, sweat, and tears into it. Being an independent forensic accountant meant I was only as good as my reputation and without a good reputation, I didn't put food on the table or keep a roof over my family's heads.

"Well." Mr. Simpson closed the file and shot me a smile. "I'll have Mary makes copies of this and as soon as the client gets here, we can begin."

"Very good."

I waited for Mr. Simpson to leave the room before sitting back down. I made sure my cell phone was on vibrate. I never totally turned it off in case there was an emergency, but I also didn't want it ringing and interrupting the meeting...unless there was an emergency.

Warmth spread through my chest as I stared down at the wallpaper on my cell phone screen. I loved that picture of Eva. She'd been hanging on a fence on the side of our little cottage by the bay, a smile on her sweet little face as she stared at me. It was one of my favorite pictures of her.

I slid my cell phone back into my pocket when I heard voices outside the conference room and stood. Time to put on my game face.

The door opened and in walked...my nightmare.

"Mr. Warner, this is Mr. Galeazzi, the new owner of—"

I turned off my laptop and slid it back into my briefcase without saying a word. I grabbed the file I'd been working on for my client and set it on the table. After closing my briefcase, I grabbed the handle and walked to the end of the table.

"I apologize, Mr. Simpson, but I am going to have to recluse myself from this meeting and I will no longer be able to work on your case. I will send all of your files back by courier as soon as I return to my office. And I will, of course, refund your deposit."

Mr. Simpson glanced between me and the man standing in the doorway, staring at me as if I had three heads. "I don't understand."

I turned to glare at Frank with all the anger and betrayal I felt, and had felt for the last five years. "I'm afraid that Mr. Galeazzi has a restraining order against me and I am not allowed within five hundred feet of him, his family, his residence, or his place of business. As such, I can no longer have anything to do with this case."

"I had the restraining order dropped as soon as I found out about it, Henry," Frank said.

"You'll have to forgive me if I don't believe you, Mr. Galeazzi. You do have a history of lying to me, after all." I nodded toward the doorway. "Now, if you'll excuse me?"

"I want to talk to you, Henry."

"No." No way, no how. I'd tried to talk to Frank numerous times and all it had gotten me was a broken heart and ten days behind bars. "Move, please."

I tried not to shout out my demand and remember that I needed to be as polite as possible, but my nerves were fraying. I had moved from one side of the country to the other to get away from Frank and here he was.

Europe sounded good.

When I went to walk past Frank, he reached for me. I instantly jumped back, holding up my arms. "Don't touch me," I snapped. "You never get to touch me."

I'd be lost if he did.

I had thought, after all these years, that I had finally gotten over Frank, but one look at his handsome face and I knew I'd just been fooling myself.

If he touched me, I might drop to my knees and beg him to finally listen to me, to explain what I had done all those years ago to make him not love me anymore. I still didn't know, and that might be what ate at me the most. I had no idea what I was supposed to have done.

I was obviously an idiot.

"Okay, Henry," Frank said slowly as if talking to a feral cat. "I won't touch you. I just want a chance to talk to you."

"I tried to talk to you. I tried so many times, I almost went insane. I even came to see you right before I moved, to beg you to talk to me. All it got me was ten days behind bars for breaking the restraining order you now say you had dropped." I narrowed my eyes. "Do you know what happens to someone like me behind bars? I can tell you, it's not pretty."

I was gratified to see the blood drain from Frank's face, but it was a small consolation to the hell I'd suffered in jail. I hadn't been raped or anything, but I hadn't walked out of jail without a few bruises. I had been terrified for my unborn child the entire time.

It was a nightmare I never wanted to live through again, and here stood the catalyst for that nightmare right in front of me.

I had to get out of here. I was almost desperate. "Please, let me leave."

Frank's lips twisted into a grimace, but he stepped back, allowing me access to the door. "We will be talking, Henry."

"Not if I can help it," I said as I hurried out of the room. I'd do just about anything to never have to deal with Francesco Galeazzi or any of his family ever again. Even if it meant giving up a lucrative contract and my good reputation.

I'd flip burgers for a living if I had to.

I tried to walk in an even stride as I made my way out of the corporate offices to the elevators, but it was all I could do not to run. I kept expecting security to jump out at me any moment and have me arrested for trespassing and violating the restraining order.

I didn't care if Frank said he'd had it dropped. I didn't trust him as far as I could throw him. The man had already proved that he was a liar and totally unreliable. I'd never believe anything that came out of his mouth.

I let out a gasp of relief when the elevator doors slid open and I was able to step inside. Alone. That was the important part. No one had followed me. Of course, as the doors slid closed, I saw Frank standing in the corridor watching me. The hard glint in his eyes told me he meant his words. We would be talking at some point.

Moving was looking better and better. I just had no idea where I could go that Frank wouldn't find me. I thought I was safe moving from one coastline to the other.

I was wrong.

I'd been so careful. I hadn't left a forwarding address. For the first year, months after Eva was born, I'd lived with Ryan and his grandmother and not put my name on anything. I'd finished my degree online. I never bought a car or renewed my driver's license. I had a P.O. Box for all my mail. No credit cards, no loans. No rental agreements. No bills in my name.

I'd done everything I could think of to not leave a trail. I never dreamed he'd find me this way. Maybe I should have looked harder at the paperwork I'd received from the company I'd been contracted to work with.

It was a standard contract. The company was being sold. They wanted a forensic accountant to go over the books and show that they were up to date and accurate. I'd done it a hundred times before. I don't remember the new owner's name being mentioned anywhere. If I'd seen it, I would have run in the other direction so fast, my shoes would have melted.

As soon as the elevator reached the first floor and the doors slid open, I stumbled out and then hurried across the lobby to the front doors. I glanced at the security station out of the corner of my eye, but the guard manning it never even looked in my direction.

Outside, I hailed a cab. It would cost a bit more than riding public transit, but I didn't think I could handle being squeezed into a bus with a bunch of other people right now.

I glanced back toward the towering office building as the cab pulled away from the curb, and then sucked in a painful breath. Frank stood outside the doors talking on his cell phone. He was staring right at me.

I quickly looked away.

My mind fluttered with anxiety, not just for me, but for Eva, too. I had tried so hard to talk to Frank, even if it was to tell him he was going to be a father. After my ten days behind bars, I decided my best course of action was to simply cut him out of our lives as if he never existed.

Of course he did or I wouldn't have Eva, and I never tried to hide the fact that she had another father from her. I especially never bad mouthed him to her even if there were times when my hatred of the man ran so deep, I felt as if my soul was black. I couldn't do that to her.

My issues with Frank were my issues, not hers. If, when she was an adult, she wanted to track her father down, that would be her choice and I wasn't about to cloud any relationship she might be able to have with Frank.

Now, he was here and I was terrified. She looked just like him so I had no doubt that the moment he saw her, he'd know she was his. I also knew, with his money, he could take her from me if he wanted to, and I couldn't think of any reason why anyone wouldn't want my sweet little girl.

I didn't realize we had stopped in front of my destination until the cab driver turned to look at me. I dug some money out of my wallet and handed it to him before grabbing my briefcase and climbing out of the back of the cab.

I glanced down both directions of the street before starting toward the little one story cottage in front of me. I wouldn't put it past Frank to have someone follow me so he'd know where I was.

I opened the front door and then let myself in. "Ryan?"

"Back here," came a reply from the back of the house.

I set my briefcase down next to the front door and then walked toward the back of the house. Ryan was in the kitchen kneading bread dough.

He smiled at me as soon as he saw me. "Hey, you're home early."

"Yeah."

I don't know what was on my face, but Ryan stopped what he was doing and rinsed his hands before walking toward me. "What's wrong?"

"Where's Eva?"

Ryan nodded his head toward the backyard. "She's out back playing with Arty. Why?"

Tears of defeat and despair flooded my eyes. "Frank found me."

Chapter Twelve

~ Frank ~

"I found him."

"Who?" Martino asked.

"Henry," I replied as I watched his cab drive away. "I found Henry."

"Where?"

"He was in the conference room when I went for my meeting this morning."

"He's in Seattle?" Sheer surprised rang through Martino's voice.

"Looks like it."

"Guess that's why we never found him. We were looking on the East Coast."

"I guess." I clenched my jaw to keep from growling in frustration. We should have searched for him on the West Coast. It was stupid not to. I'd just never thought he'd go that far to get away from me. "Did you know he came to see me right before he left? Because of that stupid restraining order you took out, he was arrested and spent ten days behind bars."

Martino's sigh was heavy. "Frank, I've apologized for that. I thought I was doing the right thing at the time. I didn't want him to hurt you anymore than he already had."

My nostrils flared as I tried to contain my rage. "Ten days, Martino."

"What do you want me to say, Frank?"

"I want you to help me find him and then you can apologize to him in person."

"Yeah, okay. I'll get our private investigator on it and then fly out there in the morning. Do you need me to do anything else?"

"No, I'll handle it."

"Are you going to try and talk with him, Frank?"

"Yes." I had to talk to him. It had been five years, but I still wanted to know why he had done what he did. Why had he slept with Ryan? Why had he stopped loving me? Why had he stabbed me in the back?

I knew I should just let it go, but I couldn't. The questions gnawed at me, keeping me up at night. It had soured me for any other relationship. I'd met a few people over the last five years, but none of them held my interest more than a couple of days or weeks.

None of them were Henry.

"I wish you luck with that," Martino said.

I didn't need luck. I had sheer determination. I wasn't going to leave Seattle until I talked to Henry and I didn't care if that took another five years.

"I need to go, Martino. I want to talk to Mr. Simpson see what he knows about Henry. Hopefully, it will give me a lead as to where he is." And where I could find him.

"Okay, I'll call you if I get an update. If I don't hear anything, I'll see you tomorrow."

"Don't tell Mama and Papa that I found Henry." They had never supported my continued search for the man they thought was a gold digger. "Just tell them you are coming out here to help me close the deal on this company."

"I got you," Martino explained. "Mum's the word."

I rolled my eyes and hung up. My brother could be quite ridiculous on occasion, but I knew he meant well. Even when he was doing something as stupid as taking out a restraining order against Henry, I knew he was doing it because he cared.

Still didn't mean I didn't want to strangle him.

I slid my phone back into my pocket and headed back into the building. I tapped my foot impatiently as I waited for the elevator take me up to the tenth floor. I had to work quickly. As freaked out as Henry had seemed, I knew he'd run at the first chance. I had to find him before he got that chance.

When the elevator doors slid open, I walked out and headed back for the conference room. Luckily, Mr. Simpson was still there, along with my assistant. "Marianne," I said in a calmer tone than I was feeling, "I'd like the room, please."

I knew better than to raise my voice to her again. I'd learned that lesson well. After I'd snapped at her one too many times, she had taken a leave of absence and threatened to quit if I didn't get my head out of my ass.

My business world had almost fallen apart two weeks after she left. After trying to hold things together—and failing miserably—I'd called her, offered her a promotion to my assistant with double the pay, and my promise to never raise my voice to her again. So far, I'd been able to keep that promise.

Today was stretching that promise very thin.

Marianne must have seen the look in my eyes because she immediately walked out of the room, closing the door behind her. I pinned my eyes on Mr. Simpson. "Tell me about Henry Warner."

"Um, well, he was recommended to me by a friend. Although he hasn't been in the business very long, he has built up a reputation for being an expert forensic accountant. He's meticulous, accurate, and turns his projects in on time."

"Who is this friend?"

"Bob Summers," Mr. Simpson replied. "Mr. Warner was the forensic accountant when Bob bought his yacht building company. He was actually able to find some inaccuracies that netted Bob over a million dollars in equity before he even signed on the dotted line."

That was pretty good.

"What are his credentials?"

"He has a degree in accounting from Washington State University and masters in finance from Southern New Hampshire University."

"No business degree?"

Mr. Simpson glanced down at the papers in front of him before shaking his head. "No, his resume only lists his accounting degrees." When he glanced up, there was a perplexed frown on the man's face. "Am I to take it you know Mr. Warner?"

"I do," I admitted, "but we lost contact a few years ago. I've been trying to find him ever since." I walked over to Mr. Simpson and held out my hand. "Can I see his resume?"

After the man handed it over, I read over it. It was actually a pretty impressive resume for someone who had only been in the business for a few years. Hell, it was an impressive resume for someone who had been in the business for a few decades. Henry had done well for himself.

"Can I take this?"

"Of course."

"We'll need to postpone our meeting until I have a chance to speak to Mr. Warner."

"Do you want me to find another accountant?"

"No, Henry will continue on the case. I just need to speak to him first."

"What about the restraining order he mentioned? That could be a problem."

"That restraining order hasn't been in effect since a few weeks after it was issued."

I could see that Mr. Simpson was dying to know why there had even been a restraining order, but I wasn't about to dredge up my life for a complete stranger. "It was a misunderstanding. My brother issued the restraining order. As soon as I found about it, I had it dropped. That's why I need to talk to Henry."

"I take it Mr. Warner was one of your employees?"

"No." I swallowed tightly before replying, "He was my fiancé."

Mr. Simpson didn't say anything, but his eyes rounded.

I carefully folded up Henry's resume and stuck it into the inside pocket of my suit. "I'll be in touch about rescheduling our meeting just as soon as I've had a chance to speak to Henry."

"Yes, of course." Mr. Simpson stood.

When he held out his hand, I shook it and then started for the door. "I'll be in town until this issue is resolved. My brother is flying in tomorrow to help me out so you might be meeting with him instead of me. Depends on how things go with Henry."

"I understand, sir."

I doubted it.

I opened the door and glanced around for my assistant. She was sitting in a chair in the hallway. "Marianne."

She stood as I walked toward her. I kept walking and she fell in beside me. "Is the meeting canceled, sir?"

"No, just postponed, although you might be taking it with Martino. I have some other business to take care of so he's flying out in the morning."

The elevator doors slid open and I stepped inside.

Marianne stepped in beside me. "Anything I can help with?"

"No, this is something I have to do on my own."

* * * *

I glanced at the quaint little stucco and brick cottage I was parked in front of. It had taken me two days, but I now knew where Henry lived, where he worked, where he shopped for his groceries, everything.

Well, everything for the last two years anyway. There was a three year gap in information where the only trace of Henry had been online while he was getting his degree from Southern New Hampshire University. I had no idea where he'd lived at the time because the P.O. Box he had listed for the school was back on the East Coast.

I took a moment to gather myself and figure out what I was going to say to Henry. I had to get him to listen to me. I had so many questions I needed to ask, so many answers I wanted, not to mention one very huge apology for what had happened to him due to that stupid restraining order.

I still had a hard time wrapping my head around the fact that Henry had spent ten days in jail. Granted, it wasn't a huge amount of time, but even a single day was too much. It never should have happened.

Once I felt I could handle my anger and keep calm, I climbed out of the car and made my way to the front door. I drew in a calming breath and then knocked. My eyebrows shot up to my hairline when the door was opened my a little brown haired boy.

"Hello," I said. "Is your mommy or daddy home?"

"My daddy is home," the kid said. "I don't have a mommy."

A niggle of apprehension exploded inside my gut. "You don't have a mommy?"

Brown hair flopped around the kid's head as he shook it.

"Is your daddy here?"

More hair flopping.

"Can I speak to him?"

"Arty, what have I told you about answering the door?" someone shouted from the back of the house. A moment later, a brown haired man walked around the corner.

I inhaled sharply when I recognized him. "Ryan."

"Frank." Anger lit in Ryan's eyes before they fell to the kid. "Arty, go play in your room and take your cousin with you. Stay there until I tell you that you can come out."

The kid ran off and Ryan faced me again. "What do you want?"

"I want to talk to Henry."

"Haven't you hurt him enough?"

I snorted rudely. "You ask me that when you're standing here in his house?"

"Our house," Ryan replied. "Henry and I live here together."

Pain instantly squeezed my heart. "You both live here?"

"We do."

When Ryan crossed his arms, I caught the flash of gold on his hand. A gold wedding band. I thought I might pass out. "Are you married?"

It was my worst nightmare come to life.

"We—"

"Go keep an eye on the children, Ryan," Henry said as he stepped around the corner. "I'll take care of this."

Ryan glared at me for a moment before turning and walking to Henry's side. "You don't have to talk to him. He can't make you."

Henry patted Ryan's arm. "It's okay. Go sit with the kids."

I could see that Ryan didn't want to. He shot me a narrow-eyed look before storming out of the room. "Thank you for agreeing to talk to me, Henry. I—"

"What did I do?" Henry asked. "What did I do to make you turn on me?"

My jaw dropped.

"You know damn well what you did."

"No, I really don't."

I waved my hand toward the hallway where Ryan had disappeared. "You were fucking Ryan while we were engaged."

There were a hundred different reactions I expected out of Henry. Laughter was not one of them.

"No, seriously," Henry said. "What did I do?"

I just stared at him until he slowly stopped laughing and his eyes began to widen.

"You're serious," Henry said. "You think I slept with Ryan."

"I know you did. I've seen the evidence."

Henry cocked his head to one side. "What evidence?"

"Damning evidence that you can't refute. Intimate pictures of the two of you together, texts between you."

Henry stared again, almost as if he was going over everything I'd said, and then he slowly nodded his head. "Okay, I guess now I know." He pointed toward the front door. "You can go now."

"Not until I have some answers."

"I don't owe you anything," Henry spat out. "I owe you less than nothing."

"I want to know why, Henry." That was the burning question I couldn't get out of my head. "I offered you everything and you betrayed me."

"I am not the one who did the betraying here, Frank."

"Well, I certainly didn't sleep with Ryan."

Henry smirked as he crossed his arms. "I don't believe you."

"You think I slept with Ryan?"

"Ryan, Stewart, whoever." Henry shrugged. "You seemed to be pretty good at lying. Why am I supposed to believe you were faithful, too?"

Wait, how did this get to be about me?

"I did not sleep with Ryan," I snapped.

"Neither did I."

"You—" I cocked my head when I spotted his gold wedding band on Henry's ring finger. "You're married?"

Henry glanced down before rubbing his thumb over the band. "Yes."

"To who?"

Henry smirked. "Ryan, of course."

I clenched my hands. Henry was lying. I just couldn't figure out why he was lying. "Tell me the truth, Henry."

Henry's eyes narrowed. "You wouldn't know the truth if it came up and bit you on the ass."

"Fine, then you tell me. What is the truth?"

"I didn't sleep with Ryan," Henry said. "I haven't slept with anyone since the moment I agreed to go out with you."

"I don't believe you."

"Yeah, whatever." Henry walked to the door and pulled it open. "You can go now."

When I turned to face him, I was brought up short by the tears in Henry's eyes. "Do you love him?"

"Who?"

Who were we talking about here?

"Ryan, of course."

Henry looked me straight in the face as he replied, "Yes, I love Ryan."

I could see the truth in Henry's eyes. He really did love Ryan. Whatever...hope maybe...that I'd been holding onto died. "Okay. Henry."

I started for the door just as a speeding little head of brown hair came flying down the hallway, past me, and barreled into Henry's arms.

"Daddy, Daddy, I hurt my finger."

Daddy?

Chapter Thirteen

~ Henry ~

Oh man, this was not going to end well.

I dropped down to one knee and drew my daughter into my arms. Using a much calmer voice than I was actually feeling, I asked, "Which finger, moppet?"

Eva held up one of her fingers. I looked it over, but couldn't see any blood or bruising, so I kissed the tip and then smiled at her. "Better?"

She nodded before resting her head on my shoulder. I could still see her looking at Frank through her lowered lashes. Eva was shy around strangers, but once she warmed up to someone, they got to see what a true ray of sunshine she really was.

I never wanted Frank to discover that.

I pressed a kiss to Eva's forehead before giving her a little push toward the hallway. "Go back and play with Arty so Daddy can finish his conversation."

Eva was a good child. She immediately ran off alike I told her to, even if she did give Frank a long look as she hurried past him. I waited until she disappeared from sight before opening the door. "You need to leave, Frank."

Frank was still looking down the hallway when he asked, "Is that your kid?"

"You know she is. You heard her call me daddy."

He glanced at me. "Where's her mother?"

"She doesn't have a mother."

Frank stared at me for a moment, his brow furrowed as if he was trying to put a puzzle together. "You're an omega?"

"You know I am." I'd never hidden that fact from him.

"Actually, no, I didn't."

My eyes widened. "You didn't know I was an omega?"

"No."

"How could you not know?" I asked. It was pretty obvious that I was an omega. I thought for sure he knew.

"We never discussed it."

"We talked about having kids."

"We talked about adopting or using a surrogate. We never talked about you carrying our kid."

Huh.

"I honestly thought you knew."

Frank shook his head. "So, if you carried her, who is her other father? Ryan?"

This was it. This was where I could end things between us once for all. It would just take a simple nod of my head. I wouldn't even have to say the word.

I couldn't do it. Not about something this important.

"No," I whispered. "I've never slept with Ryan."

Frank's eyes dropped to the ring on my finger. "So, you're not married to Ryan?"

I shook my head. "No, we're roommates. We were carrying at the same time so it made sense to pool our resources and help support each other. After I finished my degrees, it just made sense to continue living together. Ryan could watch the kids while I went to work."

"So, who's the father then?"

My spine stiffened. "I am."

"No, I mean, who is the other father, the sperm donor?"

Sperm donor. That was a good word for it.

I wrapped my arms around myself when I started to go cold. "It doesn't matter. He's not in the picture."

"Henry—"

I dropped my head into my hand and rubbed at my temples. "Please, Frank. I don't want to do this with you."

"Am I her father?"

How to answer that?

"Technically, you're her sperm donor. You are not her father." It took more than blood to make a father. It took time, commitment, love, understanding, and a willingness to be there day in and out.

"Fuck, Henry!" Frank brushed his hand over the top of his head, ruffling the ends so they stood up at odd angles. "Why didn't you tell me?"

My anger was instant and enraged. "I tried to tell you," I snapped. "I tried to email you, to call you, to message you. I even tried to go see you, and that ended with me, and your unborn child, being put behind bars for ten days."

Frank inhaled sharply. "You were pregnant when you went to jail?"

"Well, unless we slept together after that and I didn't know about it, then yes, I was."

"Fuck!"

"Stop swearing," I said. "Little ears pick up everything."

Frank's eyes darted toward the hallway. "I want to meet her."

My answer was immediate and as cold as steel. "No."

Frank swung back to look at me. "I'm her father."

"I'm her father," I countered. "You are her sperm donor." I'd already said that, but he was not her father. He was a biological part of her and that was it.

"I have a right to see her."

"You don't have any rights as far as I am concerned."

"I'll take you to court if I have to."

Those were the words I never wanted to hear, but I had expected them. "On what grounds?"

"You just told me I'm her father."

"Your name is not on her birth certificate so it's your word against mine."

"If I take this before a judge—"

"Then what? You've already said you have the proof that I was fucking around with Ryan. I have no doubt he'd swear in a court of law that he's Eva's father. There is no way you can prove a thing."

"I can get a DNA test."

"Unless I agree to it, you can only get a DNA test with a court order and you have to have a good reason to get one." I took a threatening step toward Frank, clenching my fist. "I will fight you with every breath in my body. You will not take my daughter from me."

Frank's voice softened when he spoke. "I don't want to take her from you, Henry. I just want to meet her."

"I don't believe you."

Frank's shoulders slumped.

I pressed my lips together to keep from saying something to comfort him. I was angry at Frank, enraged by what he believed, but I knew down deep in my heart that I still cared about him.

"Don't you want her to have a good life, Henry?"

"She has a good life."

"But I can help with that. I can give her a college education, a chance to see the world, whatever she needs."

"I can provide for my daughter. I've been doing it without you or the Galeazzi money since before she was born."

Frank's eyes were red rimmed and a little glossy. "Is that why you returned everything?"

"I wanted nothing from you." I snorted. It was a very rude sound, and I realized that. I just didn't care. "You Galeazzis are all so concerned about your money that you assume everyone is after it. Well, guess what? I wasn't. I never wanted any of it. I just wanted you."

I had to draw in a sharp breath and stiffen my spine when a tear trickled down Frank's cheek. He had nearly destroyed me, and he was threatening to do it again. I owed him nothing, especially not my concern.

"Do you know that the day I found out I was pregnant, I was so excited to get home and tell you? I was met at the gate to the family estate by your father. He had my bags packed and a check for five thousand dollars waiting for me and along with a message from you that you never wanted to see me again. When I refused to leave, he called the cops on me." I sucked in a painful breath. "That's the memory I have of the day I found out I carried your child."

A mire of emotions flashed through Frank's brown eyes before he glanced away and whispered, "I'm sorry, Henry."

The fight went out of me. "So am I."

He stared at me for a moment and then simply walked past me and out the front door. I held it together until I heard a car start up and peel away, and then I dropped to my knees and started silently crying.

At some point, I felt Ryan's arms come around me. I had no idea where the kids were, but I prayed they were not in the room. They did not need to see me lose it like this.

"It's going to be okay, Henry."

I seriously doubted that.

"He wants to meet her." That would be simple enough, but I knew once Frank met his daughter, he would want to be a part of her life. He wouldn't want her raised across the country for him to only have visitation rights. He'd want her with him.

I did and I'd fight to keep her.

"I don't know what I'll do if he tries to take her from me. I can't fight that. I don't have that kind of money."

"We could move again."

I shook my head. That wouldn't work either. "Now that he knows about Eva, he wouldn't stop looking for us until he found us."

"He really thinks we slept together?"

I sniffled and wiped at my runny nose as I lifted my head to look at Ryan. "You were listening?"

Ryan snorted as he settled back to lean against the wall. "Of course I was listening."

I chuckled. Of course he was. "Yeah, he says he has evidence and everything, pictures and texts. Intimate pictures."

Ryan's eyebrows lifted. "Of the two of us?"

"Yep."

"Huh." Ryan blinked madly for a moment. "Were we having a good time?"

"I don't know. Frank never showed me the pictures."

"He just accused us of having slept together?" Ryan asked. "He didn't give you a chance to defend yourself?"

"Looks that way."

Ryan snorted as he rolled his eyes. "What an idiot."

"What kills me is that if he had come and talked to me, none of this would have happened. We'd be married by now and raising our daughter together."

"You don't know that, Henry. If he's willing to believe whatever evidence he thinks he has, there's no telling what else he'd believe."

I sighed. "No, you're right. I don't see a way out of this without someone getting hurt."

"Someone has already been hurt. You."

Yeah, but in the big scheme of things, I didn't matter. My daughter did.

"Do you think I should let him see Eva?" I asked.

"Do you think he'll try to take her from you?"

"I honestly don't know."

"I think that Eva deserves to know both her parents, assuming they are both good people at heart and despite everything, you've always maintained that Frank is a good man."

"He is."

I think.

"Then, if you can get him to agree not to try and take her away from you, you give them the chance to get to know each other. They deserve that. You just have to get Frank to understand that you're the one in charge and what you say goes."

Oh, yeah, that should be easy.

Not.

"Can you watch Eva for the evening? I think Frank and I need to talk."

Ryan nodded. "Of course, but are you sure you don't want me to come with you?"

"No, this is something I need to do on my own." There were things I needed to talk to Frank about without anyone else around. Ryan was my biggest supporter. He was also my biggest defender. If Frank said the wrong thing, Ryan would go for his throat.

"You might want to clean up a bit before you go." Ryan waved his hand up and down, gesturing to my body. "You're a little wrecked right now."

I grimaced as I glanced down. "Yeah, that might not be a bad idea."

"And then you have to find him."

Damn.

I hadn't thought of that.

It didn't take me more than a few minutes to clean myself up and change into some clean clothes. It took me another two hours to find which hotel Frank was staying in, and two more after that to get up the nerve to go see him.

Frank had left and I could just let things go as they were, but I couldn't. That drive that had been inside of me all those years ago was still there. No matter what issues Frank and I had, I still felt he had a right to meet and get to know his daughter. And Eva had a right to know her father.

I wasn't sure how I felt about the rest of his family.

I walked into Frank's hotel with a clear plan in mind. I was simply going to go upstairs and tell him I would let him have a chance to meet Eva and get to know her, to be a part of her life, but only if he went with me to see a lawyer and signed something that stated he would never try to take her from me.

I almost turned and walked back out before I reached the reception desk. I clenched my hands until my nails dug into my palms and forced myself to approach the pretty young brunette behind the counter. "Francesco Galeazzi's room, please."

She smiled brightly. "Mr. Galeazzi is staying in our presidential suite on the tenth floor."

Of course he was.

"Thank you." I turned and headed for the elevators. There was a bellman standing just inside. "Tenth floor please, the presidential suite."

The young man hit a button on the wall. The doors slid closed and the elevator started moving. Sweat broke out in little pebbles across the back of my neck.

This was a really bad idea.

Chapter Fourteen

~ Frank ~

I lifted my head off the back of the couch when I heard the elevator stop on my floor. Instead of looking to see who it was, I reached for my bottle of scotch and refilled my glass. It was probably Martino or one of the hotel staff or something.

I wish it was someone to bring me a bigger bottle of scotch. I doubted the one I had was big enough for me to drown my sorrows in. I doubted there was enough scotch in the entire world, but I was certainly going to keep drinking it until I forgot the hurt on Henry's face and the knowledge that I had a little girl out there that I knew nothing about, or that I had no one to blame for that except myself.

"Frank."

I dropped the glass and turned. "Henry."

He lifted an eyebrow. "You might want to get that before it stains the carpet."

I glanced back and then grimaced as I realized scotch was spreading across the floor, staining the carpet. I quickly grabbed the glass and set it on the table before getting up and going into the bathroom for a towel.

When I came back, Henry was still standing there. I dropped the towel onto the carpet and then stepped on it to soak up the liquid. After a moment, I picked up the towel and tossed it on the coffee table and then glanced at Henry.

"Why are you here?" I never that I'd ever see him again.

"I thought maybe we could talk."

"Okay." I was a little hesitant because I simply could not figure out what we had to talk about. "Would you...uh...like a drink?"

"No, I'm good, thank you." Henry gestured to one of the chairs across from the couch. "Do you mind if I sit down?"

"No, of course, please."

Henry walked over to the chair and sat down. I sat on the couch across from him and then waited to find out why he was here.

"Okay, look, I'm just going to come out and say it. You are Eva's father and—"

"You named her Eva?"

Henry nodded. "Your grandmother was the only one who never said a bad word to me." He huffed. "She certainly never called me a well-used whore like your brother did."

I grimaced. "Sorry."

Henry waved his hand at me. "Rehashing things is not why I am here."

"Why exactly are you here?"

"Because of Eva. She has the right to get to know you. I don't want to deprive her of that."

I scooted forward on my seat, my heart starting to pound. "You'll let me see her?"

"Yes, but there has to be rules, boundaries that you'll have to agree not to cross."

"Name them." I couldn't think of anything I wouldn't do for my chance to get to know my daughter. "I'll agree to anything."

"One, you have to promise to never try to take her from me."

"Agreed."

"I know how your mind works, so I'm willing to stipulate that you can never take her from me unless you, and no less than three outside experts agreed upon by the courts, state that I am in some way harming our daughter. The same would be true for you. If three experts agreed upon by the courts deem you unsafe, your parental rights can be limited or terminated."

That was reasonable and surprisingly insightful.

"What else?" I asked.

"Two, all visitation with your family will be supervised by me or a third party. After experiencing how your family can turn on someone, and being the victim of that myself, I don't feel they are adequately qualified to care for Eva. I also have reason to believe they would try and turn her against me to get what they want."

"What about your family?"

Henry snorted. "There ain't no way in hell Eva will ever even meet my family. And if she's with you and they show up, I expect you to grab her and run."

I chuckled. "Agreed."

"Three, you may set up a reasonable college fund for her, but no gifts over fifty dollars except during holidays, and even those have to be within reason. I want Eva to grow to love you for you, and not for what you can buy her."

I swallowed tightly before answering. "Agreed."

"The same goes for your family. No trying to buy Eva's affections. She is a sweet, wonderful child who just needs to be loved. She doesn't need the next craze on TV or the crown jewels. Get her a teddy bear and spend time with her. That's what is important to her."

"Agreed."

"Four, no badmouthing each other in front of Eva. I have never once said anything bad about you in front of her and I expect the same from you and your family. Especially your family."

"Does she know anything about me?"

"She knows you exist, but she doesn't know what you look like. I didn't have any pictures of you."

"What did you tell her about why I'm not in her life?"

"When she asked why we were no longer together, I told her that sometimes parents have arguments that they can't work out and they have to go into time out for awhile and that we were both in time out from each other." Henry shrugged. "She's four. Time out is a concept she understands."

"Anything else?"

"If an issue comes up, we have to talk about it. Not Martino or your parents, but us. You and me. We have to communicate or this can all go to shit in an instant. That means you have to unblock my phone number so I can call you if I need to, and I can't be barred from coming to see you. I'll always call first, but I need to be able to see you if there's an issue."

"I unblocked your phone number five years ago when I started trying to find you, but you had changed your phone number."

"You tried to find me?"

I nodded. "After you returned everything I had given you and I learned about the restraining order, I thought we needed to talk. I went by your apartment, but you had already moved out the week before, so I went to your work and your school. You were already gone. I hired a private investigator to try and find you, but I guess I never thought you'd move all the way across the country to get away from me."

"I wasn't trying to get away from you, Frank. After I got out of jail, I gave up trying to contact you. I had nowhere to go and Ryan had offered me a way out before I went to jail, so I took it. It was a chance to get on my feet, but we had to move to Seattle."

I clenched my jaw. "Ryan, huh?"

Henry's eyes rolled. "You have got to get over this obsession you have with Ryan. I did not sleep with him."

"Then why did you move in with him?"

"Technically, Ryan and I both moved in with his grandmother, who passed away four years ago, leaving Ryan the house we live in. And, like I told you before, we were both carrying at the time and we were both on our own."

"What happened to the father of Ryan's kid?"

Henry shrugged. "One night stand."

I slumped back into the couch and dropped my head back to stare up at the ceiling. I was pretty agreeable to everything Henry had laid out. It all sounded reasonable. I just wondered how it would all work with us living on different sides of the country.

"What are you thinking, Frank?"

Henry's voice sounded closer, and I realized it was when I turned my head. He was standing beside the couch.

"I'm just trying to figure out how this will work with both of us living on different sides of the country."

Henry shrugged again as he sat down next to me. "I haven't gotten that part figured out yet. I can work anywhere, but our lives are here."

"I can visit anywhere, but my work and life is on the East Coast."

"I hear Nebraska is nice."

I chuckled. "It's flat."

"Eva doesn't start school for another year. Why don't we play it by ear until then and then we can revisit this."

"Okay."

"I know I'm asking a lot under the circumstances, but until she is a little older, I want to be with her when she visits you. I'm not saying I have to be with you every hour of every day, but I want to be there to tuck her in at night and—"

"No, that's fine. I wouldn't expect anything less. You are her father and I wouldn't take that away from you."

Henry's eyes were a little misty when he said, "Thank you, Frank."

I grabbed Henry's hand and gave it a gentle squeeze. "Thank you for letting me be a part of Eva's life. I know you didn't have to."

"Like I said, I'm not doing this for you. I'm doing it for Eva. You are her father and she has the right to get to know you. I don't want her to have to wait until she's eighteen for that to happen. You need to be a part of her life now, so she has those memories growing up."

Henry's honesty and words made something deep inside of me crack open. "Can you wait here for a moment? I have something I want to show you."

Henry frowned, looking confused. "Sure."

I got up and walked into my bedroom. I grabbed the file out of my luggage, the same one I'd asked Martino to bring with him when he flew out. After finding Henry, I had wanted to have it on hand for when I confronted him. Now, I think I needed him to help me explain it all.

Things were not adding up.

Henry's actions were not those of a gold digger. At every turn, he was telling me that he didn't want my money. He could have been pretending to be nice, but a scammer usually couldn't stick it out for five years.

I could be wrong, but I didn't think I was.

I carried the file back into the living room and took my seat again. I set the file on the coffee table before glancing at Henry. "I am not bringing these out to cause issues, but you asked to see what evidence I had." I patted the top of the file. "This is it. Do you want to see it?"

Henry licked his lips as he stared down at the file. "I'm not sure."

"Why not?"

"It feels like we just kind of settled things. I'm afraid whatever is in there might bring it all back up again."

"Would it help to know I'm starting to doubt what is in here?"

Henry's eyes snapped to mine. "Why now?"

"Because things aren't adding up. If you were the gold digger you're supposed to be, why aren't you trying to get money out of me? I'd expect child support at the very least."

"I don't want your money!" Henry stated vehemently.

"I know that. I'm just stating my reasons for starting to doubt the evidence."

Henry huffed. "Fine, let me see what you have."

I pulled out the cell phone first. Luckily, I had charged it as soon as Martino had brought it and the file to me. I had wanted to make sure I could show Henry the text messages. I turned it on and then brought up the message app before scrolling through to the damning messages.

I handed the phone to Henry.

"What am I looking at here?"

I pointed.

"Okay." Henry frowned as he read the message. He scrolled to the message above that and then the one below it. "Oh, okay, this one here? Ryan was helping me track down a gift for you. He finally found it in a little market in China town."

"What gift?"

"A jade letter opener."

"I don't remember any jade letter opener."

"That's because I never gave it to you. We broke up before I could. I still have it if you want it. It's at home in my dresser."

Strangely enough, I did.

"Okay, what about this one?" I scrolled through to the next text message. "Explain this one?"

Henry squinted at the message. "Not sure, but I think Ryan and I were studying that night."

"And he needed clothes for that?"

"He needed pajamas for that because no one sleeps naked in my apartment unless they are in my bed, and he was not."

Oh.

"This one?"

Henry squinted again, and then his face flushed. "I dented the BMW."

I glanced at the message. "Why would you be scared to tell me you dented the BMW?"

"Because, you bought it for me and it was so expensive. It must have cost thousands of dollars to fix it."

"I never actually got that dent fixed."

Henrys eyebrows lifted. "You sold it with a dent?"

Now, my face was flushing. "I never sold it. It's still in the garage back home."

I quickly scrolled through until I came to the one where I thought Ryan was telling Henry he needed to tell me about hem being in love. "What about this one?"

Henry shuddered. "This one I remember very well."

My eyebrows snapped together as I frowned. "Why?"

"Stewart was following me. It was after Martino and he filed for divorce and he moved out. At first, I just thought maybe he had a friend in the area or something, but he kept showing up wherever I was. He never said anything to me, but I know he was watching me. It was kind of creepy. I even think he might have broken into my apartment."

I frowned. "Why?"

Henry shook his head. "It's nothing I can put my finger on, but it felt as if someone had been in my apartment. Things had been moved around and were in places I don't remember putting them. Stuff like that." He shrugged. "It was nothing I could prove, so I didn't say anything."

"Stewart is the one who brought me all of this."

"I'm not surprised."

"Why not?"

"He was pretty upset that he didn't get your grandfather's ring. I've met people like him before. They'll do almost anything to get what they want, and he wanted that ring."

I held up my hand. "You mean this ring?"

"You didn't give him the ring." It didn't sound like a question, but there was a hint of amazement in Henry's voice.

"No, but I did give him five million dollars for all of this." And I was regretting that hasty decision now.

Henry's jaw dropped.

I set the cell phone down and reached for the pictures. I hesitated to give them to Henry, not because I didn't want him to see them, but because I was starting to get the distinct impression that I was a blithering idiot.

"These were what I paid for."

Chapter Fifteen

~ Henry ~

My hands were shaking as I took the stack of pictures from Frank. I wasn't sure if I wanted to see them. So far, everything Frank had shown me had been easily explained. It was a little harder to do that with pictures.

I smiled as I started going through them. They weren't as bad as I thought. Most of them were of me and Ryan studying or eating at different restaurants around my neighborhood. A few were simply of us walking arm and arm down the street.

While I could understand how someone could misconstrue them as something intimate, they weren't. Ryan was my best friend. He was the godfather to my daughter. I hugged him a lot.

It wasn't until I got to the last few pictures in the stack that I felt the bile rise in my throat. These were not the pictures of two people who were not friends.

"This isn't me," I said simply because I knew I hadn't slept with Ryan.

I wasn't even sure that was Ryan.

"Henry, it doesn't matter. I just—"

"No, I'm serious. It's not me," I said. "And it's not Ryan either."

"What?"

I grabbed the other pictures and started going through them until I found a close up of Ryan's arm. I pointed to his shoulder. "See here? Ryan has a tattoo of a sun god on his left shoulder." I picked up the fake one. "Here, in this picture, there is no tattoo. The picture has to be a fake."

I handed both pictures to Frank and then started looking through the others to see if there were anymore differences. "This one shows his tattoo also." I handed it over.

I'd been able to disprove Ryan. I needed to figure out how to disprove me. I know I hadn't slept with anyone except Frank. I just had to prove it.

I wished I had a microscope.

I went over each picture, looking them over from top to bottom. Most of them did look like me and Ryan, and probably were. It was the more intimate ones that I had an issue with simply because I was positive they were fakes. Three of them were the worst. I laid them all down on the table in front of me, side by side.

"What are you looking for?" Frank asked.

"I know this wasn't me, Frank, but you don't. I'm looking for anything on them that will prove me right."

"I've looked over these pictures a hundred times, Henry. I haven't found anything that would prove to me it wasn't you."

That's what I was afraid of.

"Can you try to look at that objectively for a minute? Instead of insisting that it's me, look for what could prove it's not me."

Frank shot me a look. "I'm not sure that's objective, Henry, but I'll look."

I was carefully looking over one of the pictures when Frank gasped. I quickly looked at him. "What?"

"Your ring," Frank whispered. "Where is your ring?"

I glanced at the picture he was looking at and then winced. It was a picture of me and Ryan, both of us naked. I was sitting behind Ryan with one hand on his chest and the other one wrapped around his dick.

"It's right there."

"No, that's my grandfather's ring. Where is the ring I proposed to you with?" Frank pointed to the ring on my finger, the one I hadn't taken off since the day he put it there. "That ring."

I grabbed the picture out of Frank's hand and brought it up close to my face. I wasn't thrilled about being eye to eye with someone's dick, but I needed a closer look. I could clearly see Frank's grandfather's ring, but he was right. There was no sign of the gold band now gracing my finger.

"I don't think that's my hand, Frank. Your grandfather's ring didn't fit, remember? We never got it resized. We meant to, but it never happened. I kept it in the black bag on my dresser. I was too afraid to lose it because it didn't fit. If someone did break into my apartment like I thought, they could have easily put it on."

Frank pulled the ring off his finger and held it out to me. "Try it on."

I grinned as I slid the ring down my finger. It clanked against the gold band. When I turned my hand upside down, the ring slid right off my finger and dropped on the floor.

"Fuck, Henry!"

"Wow." I stared down at the ring in amazement before picking it up and handing it back to Frank. "Is that the biggest I told you so or what?"

Frank slid the ring back on his finger and then buried his face in his hands. "That fucking son-of-a-bitch!"

"Who?"

Frank raised his head to glare at me. "Stewart."

"Oh no, you can't lay this at Stewart's feet. Yeah, he connived to con you out of your money, but you're the idiot who fell for it. If you'd just told him to go fuck himself, you wouldn't be out five million dollars and none of this would have ever happened."

I didn't realize how angry I was until I found myself standing over the top of Frank, shouting at him.

"I did."

"You did what?"

"When Stewart and Martino first came to me—"

"Martino?"

"Yes, Stewart went to him first and Martino brought Stewart to me."

"Why does your brother hate me so much?" I couldn't figure out what I had done to make the man hate me. I'd always been nice to him and his rat bastard of a husband. I'd never raised my voice or become physical. I just couldn't understand it.

"My brother doesn't hate you."

I flicked one finger at a time. "He believed Stewart and brought him to you instead of telling Stewart to get lost. He called me a well-used whore after trying to buy me off and telling me you never wanted to see me again. He filed the restraining order against me. How does any of this say he doesn't hate me?"

Frank glanced down at the pictures, his shoulders slumping. "I'm not sure what to think anymore."

"Do you still think that I slept with Ryan?"

"No."

At least I had that.

I picked up my old cell phone and typed in my new phone number and then set it down on the table in front of him. I stood up and then reached out to lay my hand on Frank's shoulder, giving him a gentle squeeze. "Call me when you're ready to meet Eva."

Frank grabbed my hand. "Please, don't go. Not yet."

"Frank—"

"Do you have any idea how much I loved you?"

Tears flooded my eyes, but I don't know if they were for the heartache I could hear in Frank's voice for what might have been in he'd believed in me. "I loved you, too."

There were tears in Frank's eyes when he glanced up at me. "There's been no one else. I tried a couple of times, but no one lasted more than a couple of weeks."

I smiled sadly. "I never tried. I was always too busy with Eva and I didn't want to bring someone into our lives when I didn't know if they would be sticking around."

"I'm sticking around, Henry."

I had to admit my heart sang with a little bit of joy at Frank's words, but I was worried too much had happened between us for anything more than simple friendship and caring for our daughter.

When Frank pulled on my hand, I couldn't prevent myself from following his lead until I was sitting on his lap. It was stupid—monumentally stupid—but the one thing I hadn't told Frank was that the love I'd had for him wasn't gone. It was just buried really, really deep.

"Say you forgive me, Henry." Frank's lips brushed against my temple, making me shiver. I could feel his uneven breathing blowing against my skin. His hand explored the hollow of my back as he spoke. "Say you'll give me another chance to give you, me, and Eva the life we should have had."

"Frank," I whimpered. "It's not that simple."

"It can be, if you want it to be."

Oh, I did want it. I think I wanted it more than almost anything in the world. But I wasn't the only one affected by my decision. If I fucked this up, Eva would be the one to pay for this.

"Think about what you're saying, Frank."

"I am."

"No, baby, I don't think you are." I turned and pressed my hand to the side of Frank's face. "What happens the next time someone tries to sell you pictures of me? Or one of your family thinks I'm a gold digger?"

Frank winced and glanced away. "That might have been my fault."

My eyebrows lifted. "Sorry?"

"After Stewart dropped off his evidence, I was pissed. Martino was there, and he was pissed."

I snorted. "Oh, I'm sure he was."

"I took all the evidence and went to my father."

Oh, that explained so much.

"You're not endearing me to your family here, Frank."

"No, I imagine not, but try and see it from their point of view. Many times over the years, people have tried to scam us in one way or the other. Some people have tried to sell us stuff, others have simply asked for money or donations to what they called worthy causes, which turned out to be their wallets. And other people have sidled up to us, pretending to be friends when they were not."

"Why is this always about money for you?"

"Because it's about money for other people. My family doesn't care about money beyond keeping a roof over our heads. Yes, it makes the living a little easier, but sitting down to dinner every Sunday evening is much more important to us than our next dollar."

I smiled, which seemed to surprise Frank. "Ryan and I made it a habit to sit down to dinner with the kids every night. We've been doing it since the kids could sit up in their high chairs."

"That's good. Family time is important."

"Go on with what you were saying about your family."

"When Martino was in college, he met a man named Jack. He seemed like the perfect man. He said all the right things, did all the right things, and came from a nice middle class family. My parents loved him. Well, except my grandmother. She wouldn't even speak to him. When Jack proposed, Martino was over the moon. Grandmother said she would give her blessing if Jack agreed to sign a pre-nup."

I groaned. "That fucking pre-nup."

"It's there for a good reason."

"So, what happened?"

"Martino told Jack what Grandmother said and presented him with the pre-nup. Jack went ballistic. He started going on and on about how, if Martino loved him, he would never ask him to sign anything and accusing him of setting them up for divorce by planning for what would happen if they divorced."

I'd had some of those same feelings myself.

"After Jack stormed out, Martino lost it. He started shouting at my grandmother, telling her that it was all her fault that Jack was mad at him. Grandmother simply pulled out a file and handed it to Martino. Apparently, she'd hired a detective to do a deep dive into Jack's life and it turned out that not only did he have a criminal history as long as my arm, but he had no family, and he was flat broke. He wasn't even a college student. He'd lied about everything to get the family money."

Oh man.

"That would explain the pre-nup."

"Martino almost made the same mistake with Stewart when he showed up pregnant, but he made sure the little gold digger signed the pre-nup before they got married, baby or no baby. Stewart conveniently lost the baby right after they were married."

"Conveniently? Crap, Frank, that's a horrible thing to say."

"Maybe, but I have serious doubts that Stewart was ever pregnant. It's nothing I can prove without a doctor's exam, but it seems rather easy that he miscarried right after they got married, when that was the only reason they were getting married in the first place."

"Oh."

"So, yes, my family has issues with money, but not the way you think. We work hard for our money, every single one of us. I didn't start out as CEO of my family's corporation. I started out in the mail room and I had to work my way up the ladder. I wasn't given any special treatment because I was the boss's kid either. The only thing that was ever handed to me was the position of Chief Executive Officer, and that is simply because we want a family member in that position at all times and my father wanted to retire."

"Why didn't Martino get it?"

"Martino works at the company, but he's the Director of Marketing because he leans more toward art than he does business. And he's great at it. Our marketing has gone up two hundred percent since he took over."

"So, basically, you're telling me that your family would be fine if everyone just left them alone?" I think that's what he was saying.

"Look, do you remember when I first brought you home and everyone asked if you'd signed the pre-nup?"

"Vividly."

"And do you remember how they were after that?"

I frowned as I thought back all those years ago, and then I felt a little sick to my stomach. "Yeah, they were pretty friendly after that, but that's what made it so hard when they turned their backs on me. I felt as if they had really accepted me when they didn't."

"No, they did. They adored you. It wasn't until this mess with Stewart happened that they changed. They thought, with the pre-nup, that they had provided for every eventuality, but they missed one."

I frowned. "Which one?"

"A broken heart."

Chapter Sixteen

~ Frank ~

I brushed my nose along the side of Henry's temple. "I wanted to die, Henry, and I wanted to take you with me. I was so mad at you for what I thought you had done, but I was broken, too. I felt as if my heart was being ripped right out of my chest."

It wasn't something I ever wanted to experience again, and yet I was setting myself up for a repeat. Not because I thought Henry would fool around on me again, but because I was giving him control of my heart one more time.

"I basically lost it. I started barking at people for no reason, shouting, drinking. It was bad, Henry. It got so bad, my father and brother eventually confronted me in my office and told me to take some time off. That was the same day the package from the lawyer arrived. I've been searching for you ever since."

The crinkle between Henry's eyebrows was cute. "Why were you looking for me?"

"I don't know. I guess I thought if I could find you and convince you to go to counseling or something, maybe we could work things out."

"You wanted us to go to counseling?"

"I didn't want to give up hope that we could work things out."

"Even though you still thought I had slept with Ryan?"

I sighed. "Yeah. I guess that kind of makes me an idiot, huh?"

"No." Henry's hand pressed against the side of my face again before he leaned in and brushed our lips together. "That makes you wonderful."

"How so?" I asked, hoping to get another kiss.

"Because you didn't give up on us, even with all the evidence against me. You still held out hope."

I really don't think Henry understood how much I had loved—did love—him. "I haven't been able to breathe since the moment I laid eyes on you."

I didn't give Henry time to say anything else. I knew what he needed, what we both needed. I pulled Henry close and covered his mouth with my own. I could feel Henry's shock in the sudden stiffness of his body, but then Henry melted against me, groaning as he opened his mouth to my exploration.

My calm was shattered by the hunger welling up inside of me as I explored Henry's mouth. The hard length pressed against me told me that Henry desired me just as much as I desired Henry.

I couldn't be more thrilled at the prospect.

Henry groaned, his hands tightening on my arms. I felt a low rumble build in my chest. I lowered Henry down to the couch, moving to cover the man's body with my own.

I looked down into Henry's beautiful brown eyes. I was nearly overcome with the knowledge that I held him in my arms again and that Henry was there willingly. "I want to make love to you, Henry. Will you let me?"

I could see the confusion in Henry's face, the uncertainty.

I could also see Henry's desire to give in.

"I need you, Henry," I whispered as I rubbed my finger over his lips. "Please?"

I growled low in my throat when Henry's tongue poked out to lick at my finger. I rubbed against Henry's tongue with my finger before sinking it into his mouth. I inhaled sharply when Henry's lips closed around my finger and the man began sucking on it. Each draw of Henry's mouth felt like it was mirrored on my cock.

I suddenly knew Henry was going to be big trouble for me. I had no doubt Henry could get me to come just by sucking on my finger. I'd probably pass out from ecstasy if Henry sucked on my cock. I'd barely stood it the last time.

"Yes, Frank," Henry whispered.

When his eyes rose up to meet mine, I knew I was lost. I pulled at Henry's cloths, tearing them away until the man lay naked beneath me. I needed to feel Henry's body beneath my hands. I needed to feel my body pressing down on his.

I just plain out needed.

My lips followed my hands. I kissed each inch of naked skin I had bared until Henry writhed under me, small pants and moans falling from his lush lips. And Henry had the fullest lips I'd ever seen.

"F-Frank," Henry moaned beneath me.

I immediately leaned down to take one brown hued nipple into my mouth. Henry cried out and arched up into me. I was pretty sure I'd found a sweet spot on Henry's body, one I planned to exploit to its fullest. I moved my mouth across Henry's chest to the other nipple, finding it already pert and stiff. I growled and latched onto the hard little nub.

"Frank, please, I need..." Henry wailed.

The sound of Henry pleading spiraled through me like a tornado. I quickly stripped away my own clothes then hunched over Henry's body. I grabbed him by the hips and pulled the man's body up to mine until our cocks pressed together. Henry's legs surrounded me, wrapping naturally around my waist as if they had been there a hundred times.

"I'm going to love you now, *amore mio*," I said. The dazed, wide-eyed look Henry gave me filled me with joy. I stroked my hand down his side, my eyes following, eating up every inch of naked flesh I could see. "I'm going to love you so hard."

I knew Henry had no idea how true those words really were. Henry probably thought I meant I was going to fuck him, but what would happen between us meant so much more. I had every intention of keeping him. Now that I'd found him again, I didn't plan to give him up. Ever.

I leaned down over Henry and claimed his lips again. I was mildly surprised at how eagerly Henry surrendered to the kiss, just not enough to stop. I wrapped one hand around the side of Henry's head, anchoring the man where I wanted him.

I stroked the other hand gently down Henry's side and hip. I couldn't get over how soft the man's skin felt, how wonderful it felt to touch Henry again. I shuddered slightly, overcome by the mere feeling of Henry's body pressed against mine and the knowledge I was about to claim my mate.

I licked purposefully at Henry's upper lip then delved inside to explore. I felt Henry move closer, unconsciously moving against me as if seeking more contact. Gripping Henry's hair tightly, I kissed and licked Henry's lush lips, devouring them. I would have climbed inside Henry's warm body if I could have.

As it was, I knew if I didn't get my cock in the man soon, I might pass out. My blood was pounding through my body so fast I already felt light headed. My body tingled every time it brushed against Henry's.

I hissed and jerked back when Henry bit my lips. The small nip didn't break the skin, but I almost wished it did. The smoky look of desire burning in Henry's eyes seared right through me.

"Lube," I said as I glanced around searching for something to use. "We need lube."

Fuck! Where was my lube?

"Grab the butter packet off the coffee table," Henry whispered.

I arched an eyebrow as I glanced at the table. Henry was right. There were a couple of rectangular packets of butter sitting on my dinner tray. I grabbed one and peeled it open, rubbing the butter over my fingers.

This was going to be messy.

"How do you want this?" I asked as I turned back to face Henry. "On your back or on your hands and knees?"

"I... I... I don't know." Henry blushed so beautifully when he was flustered.

I decided to make things easier for him. I reached down between us and stroked my fingers over Henry's tight puckered hole. I pressed in with my fingers, inserting one into Henry's ass.

The joy I felt when Henry's body suck me right in knew no bounds. He was made for me. I couldn't wait to feel Henry's tight body wrapped around my cock. I pushed in with another finger, scissoring them back and forth, readying Henry's body to be claimed. I would die before I let anything happen to my mate. It was my ultimate duty now to protect this man from harm, even from my own hand.

Henry pushed back when I added a third finger, his whole body moved, and his legs spreading wide. Henry looked wanton to me, desire incarnate. He looked perfect and he was all mine.

"P-Please," Henry stuttered, his head thrashing around.

I pulled my fingers from Henry's body and quickly lubed up my cock with the other butter packet. Grabbing Henry's legs, I lifted them into the air and spread them wide, baring the man's stretched hole to my hungry gaze.

Scooting forward, I watched the head of my cock press against the small puckered entrance. My hands tightened around Henry's legs as I slowly pushed into him. The sight of my cock sinking into Henry's body was astonishing.

I pushed in until my entire cock was buried in Henry's body. Henry stilled. I stilled. I glanced up at Henry to find dazed brown eyes staring back at me. Henry seemed to be holding his breath as if he waited for something.

He was, he just didn't know it.

"Mine!" I snarled savagely as I started thrusting, my cock moving quickly in and out of Henry's body. I couldn't believe how tight Henry's body felt, how wonderful the silken heat gripped me.

I was overwhelmed with the sensations shooting through my body. I leaned down close to Henry, bracing myself on my arms as I stared him straight in the eyes. "I'm going to come in your hot, tight, little ass, Henry. I'm going to mark you inside and out so that everyone knows you belong to me."

Henry blinked, his mouth falling open.

My grin was feral as I pulled back until just the head of my cock remained inside of Henry's body and then I thrust forward with all the desire I felt coursing through my body.

"Frank," Henry gasped.

"Do it, baby," I growled. "Come for me."

Henry cried out, his head pressing back into the blanket beneath him. His body arched up into me and went tense as the space between us was filled with his hot seed. Henry's hands grasped desperately for purchase, finding it on my body, wrapping around my shoulders.

One more hard thrust and I erupted, filling Henry's body with my release. I lifted my head to look down. Henry's face looked serene, an easy smile spread across the man's lips. His eyelids fluttered as if he wasn't quite conscious.

"Amore mio," I whispered softly as I gently stroked the side of Henry's face with my fingers. My heart pounded with joy, amazement, and just a hint of wonder, at what I held in my arms.

Henry's eyes fluttered until they fully opened and bright brown eyes looked up at me. "Hey."

"How are you?" I whispered. Henry's face flushed and he glanced away. I grabbed the man's chin and brought his face back to mine. "How are you, Henry? Do you hurt anywhere?"

"No." Henry smiled. "I'm good."

I smiled back. "Yes, you are."

And I was going to do everything I could to keep him.

Chapter Seventeen

~ Frank ~

I'd had a busy morning. After waking up with Henry in my arms, I had laid there and just watched him sleep for the longest time, stunned not only that he was there, but that he had stayed the night. I had high hopes for even more nights like this.

After carefully sliding out so I wouldn't wake Henry, I'd showered and dressed and then snuck out of the bedroom. I had a lot to do and very little time to do it. I started out with calling Mr. Simpson and asking him for a recommendation for a lawyer in the area, someone that could see to my needs immediately.

Once I had a name, I started making phone calls. I was hoping to have everything in place by the time Henry woke up or soon after, but my plans were interrupted by the arrival of my brother. I almost growled at Martino when I opened the door and saw him standing there.

"What do you want?"

Martino's eyebrows lifted as he chuckled. "Well, hello to you too, brother."

I rolled my eyes and turned and walked away. I heard the door close behind me, but I wasn't stupid enough to think Martino had left. I was just glad I'd cleaned up the living room this morning. Henry's clothes were neatly folded on a chair in the bedroom and the butter packets had all been cleaned up.

"I'm expecting company," I told Martino. "I'm a little busy right now."

And I really didn't want Martino here when Henry woke up. I could understand Henry's anger and disdain at Martino, and I even understood that animosity, even if I didn't think it was true. Martino cared about me and his actions were based on that, not on a desire to keep me and Henry apart.

"Anything I can help with?"

"No."

"Oh, well, I just came over to talk to you about the merger. I met with Mr. Simpson like you wanted me to. I'm not sure of everything I was looking at so I brought the file for you to look over before I signed."

That actually made sense. Martino didn't do business acquisitions and mergers. That was my department. Maybe I could give it a quick look over and get Martino out the door before Henry woke up.

I held out my hand. "Let me see the file."

Martino set his briefcase down on the table and opened it up. He grabbed a file out of it and handed it over. I set the file down on the table and started flipping through it. Everything on the surface looked good, but I wished Henry had had a chance to go over it before now. I really didn't feel comfortable signing without having a forensic accountant go over the accounts.

Technically, it wasn't too late to hire him for the job, and I knew the money would be going to a good place. The care of my daughter.

"Leave this here with me," I told Martino. "I'll go over it better a little later."

"Okay, well, I'm supposed to meet with Simpson again in a couple of days."

"I should be done going over it by then." And hopefully, Henry would, too.

I clenched my jaw when Martino made himself a cup of coffee. I should have offered, but I hadn't wanted Martino to stay.

"So, did you find him?"

"Who?" I asked, playing dumb.

"Henry, of course."

I sighed because I couldn't lie to my brother. "Yes."

"And?" he asked. "What happened?"

"A lot, actually." I closed the file and pushed it away before leaning back in my chair. "Did you know that the pictures were fakes when you brought them to me?"

Martino's mouth started to drop open before he snapped it closed. "Is that what he told you?"

"That's what he proved to me." I got up and walked over to my briefcase and grabbed the photographs I'd purchased from Stewart. I tossed them down onto the table in front of Martino before taking my seat again. "Take a look at them. Pay special attention to the ones of Ryan and Henry in bed together."

"Frank, I don't want to see—"

"Look at them!"

Martino heaved a breath, but grabbed the stack of photos and started going through them. "Okay, so what am I supposed to be seeing here?"

"It's what you're not seeing."

"Come again?"

I grabbed the main photo, the one where Henry's hand was supposedly wrapped around Ryan's dick. "No wedding band."

"What?"

"When I proposed to Henry, I used a simple gold wedding band. It isn't in that picture. You can see the two rings in other pictures, just not those three."

"So? He took it off."

"Also, in the pictures that ring fits Henry's finger perfectly." I held up my hand and showed Martino Grandfather's ring. "This does not fit Henry. It's way too big. We were supposed to get it sized, but never got around to it. Henry kept it on his dresser, only wearing it occasionally."

Martino's eyebrows drew together as he frowned and glanced down at the photograph again. "I don't understand."

"It's very simple. That isn't Henry, but it's not Ryan either."

"What? His ring doesn't fit either?"

"I have no idea, but Ryan has a tattoo on his left shoulder. Where's the tattoo in these pictures?" I picked up a few of the others; the ones Henry had admitted were actually him and Ryan. "You can see it here, and here, and here, but there is no tattoo in any of these three pictures."

The more intimate pictures.

"Maybe he covered it up."

"Really, Martino?" Just how far was Martino going to push this, and why was he pushing so hard? Maybe Henry was right? "Why are you so insistent that Henry was unfaithful to me? Why do you hate him so much?"

"I don't hate him," Martino insisted.

"Seems to me you kind of do. You've certainly done everything you can to try and keep us apart. You even issued a restraining order against him when I never asked for one." I clenched my hands into fists as I leaned forward in my chair. "Did you know Henry was carrying my child when you had him arrested and thrown into jail?"

Martino gasped as his eyes rounded. "Your child?"

"Yes, my fiancé and my unborn child spent ten days behind bars because of that stupid restraining order."

Martino's face became and emotionless stone mask. "How do you know he isn't lying? How do you know he was even pregnant?"

"I know because I've met my daughter!" I snapped.

All of the blood drained from Martino's face. "Your daughter?"

"Henry didn't say he was pregnant to try and trap me into marriage. We were already engaged, remember? And he had signed the pre-nup and everything. He was not after our money. He wants nothing to do with our money."

"He may say that, but—"

I slammed my fist down on the table as I snarled, "Henry is not Stewart or Jack, Martino."

Martino's lips pressed into a thin line as he leafed through the pictures again before tossing them onto the table. He looked me straight in the eyes before asking, "Are you really sure he's telling you the truth, Frank?"

"Yes," I said without hesitation.

"Then I don't know what to tell you. Everything I saw said Henry was in the wrong here, but now you're telling me he wasn't. I don't understand how that works. How can you simply dismiss all of this? What about the text messages?"

"Henry and I had a long talk last night. He explained all of this and he made me see a few things. Stewart took a series of events, none of which would be questionable unless you were looking for something to pin on Henry, and tossed them all together, making him look guilty."

I had to search for the words to explain to Martino what I was just coming to terms with. "We were so worried about someone coming after our money that we automatically assumed someone was guilty without proof, so when evidence was presented to us, we could point our finger and crow that we were right. It was guilty until proven innocent." I shook my head in disgust at my own actions. "Henry never had a chance."

I grabbed the stack of pictures, the innocent pictures, and started slamming them down on the table one at a time. "Ryan and Henry were friends and study buddies. They spent a lot of time together. They studied together, they went out to eat together, and Ryan even brought his pajamas over to sleep on Henry's couch when they would study late into the night. These are all things friends do together."

I picked up the three more intimate pictures. "But if you add these pictures, there is a clear line of evidence of someone in a relationship."

"And the text messages?"

"All explained." I pointed a finger at Martino. "And one of them was Ryan telling Henry he needed to tell me that he'd spotted Stewart following him."

"You really think Stewart set him up?"

"I think that Stewart was after our money and when he couldn't get it through you, he came up with another way to get it. I also think none of us ever gave Henry a true chance because we were always waiting for the other shoe to drop, and when it dropped right into our laps, we knew we were right and Henry was guilty."

My burst of laughter was a cold sound, but I felt cold all the way to my soul. "I never gave Henry a chance to defend himself. I just assumed he was guilty. He didn't even know what he'd been accused of until yesterday."

"Fuck, Frank, are we that twisted?"

"Yes." I drew in a shaky breath. "And my punishment is the knowledge that I missed the first four years of my daughter's life because of my stupidity. I missed four years that I could have had Henry at my side, building a life with him and Eva."

"Eva?"

"Henry named our daughter after our grandmother because he said she was the only one who never said a hard word to him."

"Fuck." Martino pressed his fingers against his eyes before dropping his hand to the table. "This is going to kill Mama and Papa."

"And that's their punishment." They had missed out on the same four years as me. "Henry has agreed to let me see Eva, but he doesn't want any of you around her without supervision. He doesn't trust any of you." I was pretty sure he didn't trust me either, but I was working on that. "He doesn't want you around her at all."

"He...He hates me that much?" Martino whispered.

"He says he doesn't hate you, but he certainly doesn't trust you."

"I guess I haven't given him much of a chance to."

"None of us have. We were so concerned with making sure that no one took our money that we forgot people are innocent until proven guilty. Henry did everything we asked. He signed the non-disclosure agreement, he signed the pre-nup after making sure he had absolutely no access to our money, and he turned down every chance he had to get that money. And we still turned on him."

"So, what are you going to do now?"

"Hopefully, get to know my daughter and see if I can convince Henry to take me back."

Martino's eyebrows lifted. "You're going to try and get him back?"

"I want my family, Martino, and that includes Henry and Eva both."

That was all that was important now.

Chapter Eighteen

~ Henry ~

The loud voices in the other room woke me. It took me a minute of looking around to realize where I was and what had happened last night. I sat up and then rubbed my hands over my face. Well, at least Frank had moved me to the bedroom before anyone saw me, but I still had to do the walk of shame to get out the hotel room.

I glanced around until I spotted my clothes carefully folded in a stack on a chair by the door. I slid out of bed and walked into the bathroom before getting dressed. I needed to splash some water on my face and pray that there was a brush I could use. I might have to wear yesterday's clothes, but I could at least try to look human.

As soon as I was done in the bathroom, I walked back into the bedroom and got dressed. Frank had even brought my shoes in, which was a huge plus.

I could still hear voices from the other room, but they weren't as loud as they had been when they woke me up. I was assuming, whoever Frank was talking to, he'd told them to lower their voice.

I walked over to the door and cocked my head to one side and tried to listen, to hear who Frank might be talking to. Nope, I didn't have a clue. Knowing I had no other choice, I pulled the door open and stepped out of the bedroom.

Two men instantly turned to face me. One I wanted to see. One I hoped never to see again. I ignored Martino and walked up to Frank. "I need to get back."

"Can I come over?" Frank asked.

I nodded. I knew he'd want to come meet Eva sooner rather than later, and I kind of did, too. "Why don't you come a little before lunch? We can go to the park and play and then have lunch when we get back."

Frank grinned before leaning down to brush our lips together. "I'd like that."

I grinned back. "I'll see you then."

I started toward the door without saying a single word to Frank's brother. I really had nothing to say to him, at least nothing nice.

"Not going to say hello, Henry? That's rather rude, don't you think?"

I swung around and smiled sweetly. "Well, you know us well-used whores, Martino. We tend to be rude."

I was so anxious, I was surprised I made it into the elevator without tripping over my feet. It helped that Martino was staring at me with his mouth hanging open. Frank was just smirking as if he was enjoying the whole thing.

I waved to Frank as the elevator doors slid closed and then slumped back against the wall. I would have liked to spend more time with Frank, but I really did have to get back. Ryan said he'd watch Eva for the evening and that had ended several hours ago. I knew he'd do it anyway, but I should have asked. Now, I had to go home and explain to him why I was so late getting home.

That was going to be a fun conversation.

I was feeling a little more anxious when I stepped off the elevator, so when I spotted a head of blond hair I almost dismissed it, until I heard the man speak and then a cold black fear slid up my spine.

"I'd like to know which room my husband is in," the blond demanded

"Certainly, sir," the receptionist replied. "Can I see some ID?"

The blond huffed and dug out his ID, handing it over. The receptionist looked it over before handing it back. "Sir, I have two Galeazzis registered in the hotel. Francesco Galeazzi and Martino Galeazzi."

The blond gasped. "Francesco is here?"

"Yes, sir. He's in the penthouse suite."

"And Martino? Which suite is he in?"

"He's room seven-twenty."

"Not a suite?" the blond asked.

"No, sir."

"Can you tell me if Mr. Trevor Franklyn has checked in yet?"

"I'm afraid I can't give out that information, sir."

"Can I leave him a message?"

"Of course." The receptionist handed over a pad of paper and a pen.

The blond wrote down a message and then handed the pad and pen back. "Please tell Mr. Franklyn that I will be in the bar waiting for him."

With a flounce, the blond turned and walked away, and that was when I knew who he was. I darted back into the elevator and hit the button for the top floor several times. I didn't let out the breath I was holding until the doors slid closed without anyone else stepping in.

Frank and Martino were still sitting at the small dinette when the elevator doors slid open and I stumbled out. Frank stood as soon as he saw me and started across the room.

"Henry, what's wrong?"

"Stewart is here."

"What?" Frank nearly shouted.

"I just saw him downstairs in the lobby. He was at the reception desk asking what room his husband was in. The receptionist demanded he show ID, which he did, and then she told him what rooms you both were in. He seemed surprised that you were here, Frank."

Frank wrapped an arm around me when he reached me and then turned to look at his brother. "Is there some reason why Stewart would be here looking for you?"

"No," Martino said quickly, almost too quickly. "I haven't seen Stewart since the night he stormed out of your office. I didn't even see him when I went to sign the divorce papers."

"Then why is he here?" Frank demanded to know.

"Uhm, he might not actually be here to see Martino," I said. "He asked for another man, someone named Trevor Franklyn. When the receptionist refused to tell him anything, Stewart left him a message and said he would be waiting for him in the bar."

"Trevor Franklyn." Frank frowned. "Where have I heard that name before?"

Martino's face flushed red and his hands clenched as he stood. "Trevor Franklyn was Stewart's divorce attorney."

"You don't think he hooked someone else, do you?" Frank asked.

"If there's money involved, then yes. Stewart has proven time and time again that he will do whatever he has to do to get his hands on other people's money."

I would have felt bad about what Martino was saying, considering he'd said something just like that to me, but then I remembered what Stewart had done to me and Frank, and anger ran roughshod over any misgivings I might have had.

"We can't allow him to take some other poor sop to the cleaners," I insisted. "He's taken enough."

"The five million dollars he got from me should have lasted him a lifetime," Frank said.

"If you add in the five million he got from me in the divorce," Martino said, "then he had enough to last him into the afterlife."

My eyes rounded. "He got ten million dollars from you guys?" No wonder they had issues with money. They were losing it left and right. "You might want to think about changing the amount in the pre-nup from here on out, to like a hundred dollars or something."

"You wanted ten million," Frank insisted.

"Yeah, but only if you were unfaithful to me. If we were just getting divorced or I was unfaithful, I didn't get anything, but if you were unfaithful, I wanted you to pay through the nose. Money seems pretty important to you and I wanted you suffer if you were ever unfaithful to me. I figured that was the easiest way to go about it."

Frank chuckled as he tightened the arm he had wrapped around my waist. "I think it would have been less the knowledge that I lost ten million dollars that would have made me suffer, but more that I would have lost you."

I smiled up at Frank. "That's a really nice thing to say."

"Guys, guys," Martino said, "can we concentrate on what's going on with Stewart?"

"We don't know what's going on with Stewart," Frank said. "He was asking for you, telling the receptionist that he was your husband. What do you know about that?"

"Nothing," Martino said. "Like I said, I haven't seen Stewart since that night he brought the pictures and stuff to your office. I haven't even heard from him or seen him in passing. It was like he fell off the face of the earth, and frankly, I didn't care if he did."

"Then why is he still saying he's your husband? I know the divorce went through. I filed a copy of your divorce decree in the family legal file myself."

"Well, he obviously knows you are here," I said. "The question is how and why would he care? Is there anything you could have said or done that would make him think he might have a second chance with you?"

Martino snorted. "Hell, no!"

Martino said it so vehemently that I had to believe him. "He's obviously here to start trouble." It was the only reason I could think of for him to be asking for Martino's room. "Now, you guys can keep throwing more money at this gold digging moron, you can ignore him, or you can deal with him. It's your money so you have to make that decision, but I still have to get home to my kid. I've been gone long enough."

Before anyone could say anything, the house phone rang. Frank walked over to pick it up. "Hello?" He listened for a minute before his eyes darted to me and then Martino. "No, that will be fine. Send him on up."

I lifted an eyebrow when he hung up. "Who was that?"

"That was the front desk letting me know that the lawyer I hired is here."

I frowned as a spark of apprehension ignited in my gut. "What do you need a lawyer for?"

"I wanted to draw up some paperwork concerning those boundaries we talked about last night. I wanted you to know I was serious about agreeing to them."

I sucked in a breath. "The boundaries I listed?"

Frank shrugged. "I figured if I wrote something up, signed it, and filed it with the courts, you'd know that I actually do agree to your stipulations and it might relieve some of your worry."

I didn't know whether to laugh or cry. "Thank you, Frank."

Frank started to smile, but his face was also flushing red so I was hesitant and confused. I narrowed my eyes. "What aren't you telling me?"

"I asked him to update the pre-nup and bring it with him."

I waited for the anger to hit me, for the disbelief that Frank could actually think I'd sign that stupid pre-nup again. I waited to feel disbelief at the gall of the man to assume I was even interested in marrying him again.

None of it happened.

"Okay."

Frank's eyebrows shot up. "Okay?"

"Yeah."

"You'll sign it? I mean, we don't have to get married right away or anything, but I thought if the money thing was off the table all together, it would allow us to spend time together while I'm getting to know Eva without either of us constantly worrying about the money part of things."

"No, it makes sense, as long as you understand that this engagement is penciled in, not written in stone. Our lives have changed a lot in the last five years, and so have we. We might not even like each other anymore."

"What we did on the couch last night proves otherwise."

Martino quickly moved away from the couch.

"No," I countered, "what we did on the couch proves that sex has never been an issue for us. It's when we actually have to converse that we fuck things up."

Frank nodded as if saying "Yeah, maybe".

"I did change one thing in the pre-nup," Frank said out loud. "I added natural born children to the fifty-fifty custody part of the agreement, but it will only go into effect if we get married and then divorced."

I wasn't sure how I felt about that. I'd have to give it a little thought. Eva had been mine since before she was born. I wasn't sure I was willing to share custody yet. "I'll have to think on that one, Frank."

"I understand that, but, remember, this only goes into effect if we get married and then divorced. If we get married, we'd share custody anyway. This clause is to protect both of us and Eva."

"No, I get that." I just wasn't sure how I felt about it.

There was a knock at the door before anyone could say anything else. When Frank started walking toward it, Martino motioned to the balcony. "I'm going to step outside and make some phone calls, give you guys a little privacy."

I nodded simply because I didn't know what to say to that. I turned to face Frank when he opened the door to two men. A man in a dark navy suit who looked to be in his mid-fifties stepped inside, holding out his hand.

"Mr. Galeazzi, I'm Harold Evans, the lawyer you requested." He waved his hand to the other man, also in a dark suit, but looking about twenty years younger. "This is my associate, Trevor Franklyn."

Oh, shit!

Chapter Nineteen

~ Frank ~

I shot Henry a quick look before shaking both men's hands. "Please, come in." I waited until they walked past me before closing the door and walking over to stand next to Henry. "This is my fiancé, Henry Warner."

Henry stayed where he was, but nodded to both men. "Gentlemen."

"Why don't we sit down?" I grabbed Henry's hand and drew him over to the couch. I took a seat and pulled him down beside me. I did not let go of his hand. "Did you bring the papers I requested?"

"Yes." Mr. Evans set his briefcase on the coffee table and opened it up. He pulled out a large legal sized folder and handed it over to me. "I believe this is what you requested?"

I felt Henry scoot closer as I flipped the folder open and began reading. After I finished reading each page, I handed it to Henry. When I got done, I could only find one thing that needed to be changed.

"The payout amount if I am unfaithful is supposed to be ten million dollars, not five."

I heard a small gasp, but I wasn't sure who it came from.

"Do you have a pen?"

"Yes, of course." Mr. Evans handed me a pen. I crossed out the wrong amount and wrote in ten million dollars, and then initialed it before handing it off to Henry. He read it over and put his initials next to mine before handing it back.

"If you are agreeable to the terms, and have some form of valid identification, I can notarize them, and then we wouldn't have to have them rewritten and taken down to the office. I am certified in this state."

I glanced at the man beside me. "Henry?"

Henry nodded. "That would be fine, but is there any way we can get two copies notarized? One for me and one for you?"

"I can ask if they have a copy machine at the front desk," Mr. Franklyn said. "You'd have to sign both copies, of course."

"I'm agreeable to that," Henry said.

"Trevor, could you grab the small case in the backseat of the car," Mr. Evans said as he dug his keys out of his pocket and held them out. "I seem to have forgotten it."

Trevor grabbed the keys, and the folder, and then headed for the door.

I waited for the door to close before looking at Mr. Evans. "Does Mr. Franklyn work for you?"

"Yes, Trevor became one of the lawyers in my firm about a year ago when he moved to Seattle with his husband."

"His husband?"

"Yes, a nice young man named Stewart."

"Trevor is married to Stewart?" Martino snapped as if he had been standing right outside the door listening.

Mr. Evans spun around.

"This is my brother, Mr. Evans. Martino Galeazzi. Martino, this is Mr. Harold Evans, the lawyer I hired to facilitate the paperwork for Henry."

"Trevor is married to Stewart?" Martino asked again.

Mr. Evans nodded. "Yes."

Martino pulled out his phone and swiped his finger across the screen several times before turning the screen toward the lawyer. "Is this Stewart?"

Mr. Evans frowned as he looked at the picture. "Yes, but..." He glanced at me and then Henry before looking back at Martino. "How do you have a picture of Trevor's husband?"

"Because he used to be my husband and Trevor was his divorce attorney."

"I don't...I don't understand."

"It's like this, Mr. Evans," I said. "We have a conflict of interest here. Trevor Franklyn was the divorce attorney for my former brother-in-law and is now married to him. I do not believe it is ethical for him to work on our case."

"No, of course not." Mr. Evans straightened his tie and then smoothed down the lapels of his suit. "I can recommend another associate in our office, or if you would feel more comfortable, another firm for you to work with."

"I have a question," Henry said. "Did Trevor know who you were coming to see today before you arrived?"

"Uh, yes, he is a junior lawyer in the firm so he worked on the file for me."

"So, he knew he was working on paperwork for Francesco Galeazzi and me, Henry Warner?"

Mr. Evans started to look a bit nervous. "Yes, I believe so."

"While Francesco Galeazzi is quite the unusual name, and with the name Henry Warner added in, I doubt he could have been confused. He had to know it was a conflict of interest."

Mr. Evans swallowed tightly. "I assure you, I was totally unaware of any of this. Trevor never said anything to me. I certainly would not have had him work on the case or accompany me today if I had even the slightest indication that—"

"Did you know Trevor's husband is downstairs in the lobby right now?" Henry asked. "I was in the lobby when he arrived. He asked for their room, saying he was Martino's husband. Then he left a note for Trevor to meet him in the bar."

"You should also know that Stewart conned me out of five million dollars," I added in. "He said he had evidence that my fiancé had been unfaithful to me and showed pictures that we know were doctored."

"And that was after he got five million dollars out of me when we divorced," Martino said. "In a word, Stewart is bad news, and I'm pretty sure Trevor is in this up to his neck."

Mr. Evans pulled a white handkerchief out of his pocket and began mopping his face. "This is going to ruin me."

"No, it's not," Henry said. "If you didn't do any of this, then you have nothing to worry about, but if we find that you did, if you knew anything, I will personally destroy you."

"Please, I knew nothing." There was a hint of desperation in Mr. Evans' voice. "I swear."

"I don't want to bring the police and the courts into this unless I have to, Mr. Evans," I said, "but I will if I have to. I need to know everything you know about Trevor Franklyn and his husband."

"It's not that much, I'm afraid. I didn't hire him and he's just one of a bunch of lower level lawyers we have in the firm. He was the one available when you hired me."

"What can you tell us about his past?" I asked. "Where's he's from? Who his references were? Any interactions you might have had with Stewart? Anything at all that you can think of."

Mr. Evans started talking, but it quickly became apparent that he really didn't know much. He'd only interacted with Trevor a couple of times due to work and Stewart at a couple of company parties.

"Is there any way you can get me a copy of his resume?"

"Give me a moment and I'll have my secretary email it to me."

"Actually, can you have your secretary email it to this email?" Henry quickly wrote an email address down on a piece of paper and then slid the paper across the table to Mr. Evans.

While Mr. Evans made his phone call, I turned to look at Henry. "What's your take on this?"

"I think Trevor and Stewart are working together and have been working together for quite some time. I just can't figure out what their game plan is."

"We know they are after money. It's always been about the money, but if they think they can fool me with fake pictures again, they're stupider than I thought." I'd almost lost Henry once due to them. I wasn't about to let them do it again.

Icy fear twisted around my gut when Henry gasped and reached for his phone. "Henry?"

Terror, stark and vivid, glittered in his eyes when he raised them to meet mine. "Eva."

Fear and anger knotted inside of me. "Call Ryan, check on her."

"That's what I'm doing." Except his hands were shaking and he could barely dial. I took the phone from him and punched in the number and then put the phone on speaker so we both could hear what was going on.

"Hey, man, when are you getting home?" Ryan asked. "Eva is starting to get worried."

"Ryan, this is Frank. Is everything okay there?"

"Yeah, everything is fine."

I gripped Henry's hand. "Where is Eva?"

"She and Arty just finished breakfast. I sent them to their room to play while I clean up."

"Can you check on them?"

"What's going on, Frank?" Ryan asked. "Where is Henry?"

"Just do it, Ryan," Henry shouted. "Please."

"Okay, okay. You'd think after a night spent out with Frank that you'd be in a better mood."

I could hear Ryan walking and a moment later, a door opened and the sounds of kids came through the phone.

"Hey, Eva, Daddy is on the phone."

"Daddy?" I smiled at the excitement in Eva's voice and hoped that one day she'd be just as excited to talk to me. "Hi, Daddy, when are you coming home?"

Tears swam in Henry's eyes as he smiled up at me. "Soon, poppet, and I'm bringing a surprise for you."

"What is it?" Eva asked.

"If I told you," Henry countered, "then it wouldn't be a surprise."

The relief I felt almost took the breath out of me. I was ready to turn this whole fiasco over to Martino so I could go see Eva with my own eyes and assure myself that she was okay.

"Feel better?" Ryan asked.

"I'll explain this all to you when I get home, Ryan," Henry said, "but things have been a little insane."

Ryan snorted. "You didn't have to get two kids up, dressed, and to the breakfast table by yourself. That's insane."

"Look, I'm going to be bringing Frank back with me to meet Eva. We're going to go to the park for a little while and then have lunch together. You and Arty are welcome to join us. We are going to the park after all."

"We might join you at the park so Eva has someone to play with, but I think we can find somewhere else to be while you guys all have lunch. Maybe I'll take him to that burger place down the street."

"Seriously, Ryan," Henry said, "its okay if—"

"Hold on, someone is at the door."

"No!" Henry grabbed the phone and started shouting at it. "No, don't answer the door, Ryan. Just stay inside and call the—"

Two shots rang out and then the kids started screaming.

"Ryan! What's going on?" Henry screamed. "Ryan!"

"Hello, Henry," someone said who was definitely not Ryan.

"Wh-Who is this?"

"That's not important. Is Frank there?"

I knew who it was. "What do you want, Stewart?"

The chuckle that came from the man was evil and dark. "Which one of these little darlings is yours, Frank? The boy or the girl?"

Henry gasped.

"They're both mine," Frank said.

"Twins? How delightful. Well, in that case, I want five million dollars for each of these little lovelies or you will never see them again. I also want use of the family jet, destination to be determined by me once I am onboard."

"Done," I said instantly.

"No cops, no feds, or they die."

My jaw clenched. "Understood."

"You might want to call an ambulance for Ryan so he doesn't bleed out all over the floor."

Fuck!

"Wait, how do I get the money to you?" I asked.

"I'll call and let you know."

The line went dead.

Henry lost it, screaming at the top of his lungs as huge tears slid down his face. I grabbed him and pulled him into my arms, pressing his head against my chest even when he fought me.

"Martino, call an ambulance and send it to Henry's house and then call Mama and Papa and let them know what is going on."

"What exactly is going on?"

"Call the fucking ambulance, Martino!"

If Ryan died, I'd never forgive myself.

I waited until Henry's cries had lessened to the occasional sob and then cupped his face and tilted his head back so I could look at him. "I will get our daughter back, Henry. I swear I will."

"Arty," Henry whispered.

"Arty, too." I stood up and then pulled Henry up beside me. "Mr. Evans, I'm sorry, but you're going to have to stay here until the police get here and they can take your statement. You can order whatever you want from room service."

"Of course," the lawyer replied.

"They said no police," Henry whispered.

"They always say no police, Henry." Besides, I wasn't exactly calling in the police. "But I don't want you to worry about that. We need to get over to the house as fast as we can. We need to make sure Ryan is okay."

I stuck Henry's phone into my pocket. I wanted to be able to hear it if Stewart called back. "Come on, Martino." I would have preferred leaving him here to keep an eye on Mr. Evans, but I needed him with me to run interference with anyone who might try and get in our way or not listen to us. He might be the only thing keeping me from strangling people.

The elevator seemed to take forever and by the time we got outside the hotel, I just hailed a cab. I didn't have time to go looking for my car. I ushered everyone inside, gave the driver the address. "Two hundred dollars if you can get us there fast."

The cab shot out into traffic. The driver made good time, especially considering the traffic. He pulled up in front of the house next to Henry's fifteen minutes later. I handed the driver our fare plus the two hundred dollars I'd give him. I held up another hundred dollar bill. "If you can stick around, we might need another ride."

"You got it, man."

I slammed the door shut after Henry and Martino had climbed out and then assessed the situation in front of me. There was no ambulance. I hoped that simply meant they had already left with Ryan. There were, however, a lot of cops.

I walked up to the closest one. "My name is Francesco Galeazzi. That's my fiancé's house."

"Can I see some ID?" the officer asked.

The three of us pulled out our wallets and showed the officer our IDs.

The officer grimaced as he handed them back. "I'm afraid there's been a shooting, sir."

"I know," I said quickly. "We were on the phone with Ryan when he was shot. I want to know if there are any signs of the kids."

The officer's face paled. "Kids?"

"Two, both four years old. One named Eva Warner. One named Arty—"

"Arturo Jones," Henry said. "We call him Arty."

I glanced down at Henry. "Ryan named him after my grandfather?"

Henry shot Martino a quick look before whispering, "We'll talk about it later."

Right.

"After Ryan was shot, we heard the kids screaming, and Henry had just gotten off the phone with Eva, so we know they were here."

"Hold on while I get the detective in charge."

Henry waited for the officer to walk away before looking up at me again. "How could Stewart tell us to call an ambulance for Ryan and not expect the police to be involved in this mess?"

"Simple," I said. "He's an idiot."

I don't think he understood how much this act of insanity was going to bite him in the ass.

Chapter Twenty

~ Henry ~

I felt as if I was going to unravel at any moment. There were all of these police going in and out of my house, people dusting for prints, and the constant barrage of questions from the detectives. It was like no one was out searching for Eva, for my baby. They were all here in my house.

It was maddening.

I wanted Eva and Arty found. My heart was breaking, splintering into a million little painful pieces, and the only one who could understand what I was feeling was currently in surgery, fighting for his life.

"Here, baby, drink this."

I automatically drank the soda Frank handed me. I didn't even question why I was drinking a soda. I didn't care.

Frank squatted down in front of me. "How are you doing?"

"I want my baby, Frank. I want Eva."

Pain glittered in Frank's deep brown eyes. "I know, and I'm doing everything I can to find her. I already have the money set up to give to Stewart when he calls."

I swallowed tightly and glanced down at my hands. "Do you think he'll give them back once he has the money?"

"I don't know."

I could hear the hesitation in Frank's voice and knew he hated saying that to me. I sent him a small smile. "Thank you for not lying to me." I glanced up when one of the detectives walked over to us. "Has there been any word? Did you find them?"

"No, not yet, but we're working on it," the man said. "I just wanted you to know the hospital called and your friend Ryan is out of surgery. The doctor says he has a bit of a recovery ahead of him, but he should make a full recovery."

"Oh, thank god." Frank caught me when I leaned into him. I closed my eyes for a moment, my relief beyond what I could handle. I'd lived with Ryan for five years. He was my best friend. When I opened my eyes, I looked back up at the detective. "Does Ryan know about Arty?"

"Not yet." The man shook his head. "He's still in recovery."

"I should be the one to tell him." I didn't want to, but it would be better coming from me than some random police officer.

"The doctor said he should be asleep for the rest of the night. I can arrange for an officer to take you up there first thing in the morning."

"Thank you."

I jumped when my phone started ringing. Frank had been carrying it his pocket, but when the police learned that this was a kidnapping as well as a shooting, they had taken it and hooked it up to a machine that was supposed to record the call as well as help track it.

Frank jumped up and ran to the table where the phone was located. I raced after him. I'm pretty sure my heart had frozen in my chest.

"Now, remember," the detective said as he grabbed a headset and held it to his ear. "Try to keep him on the line as long as you can. The longer he talks, the better chance we have of tracking him."

Frank nodded before answering the phone. "Hello?"

"I told you no cops, Frank."

"You had to know they were going to get involved, Stewart. You were the one to tell me to call an ambulance for Ryan. He was shot. The cops don't let things like that go without investigating."

"You broke a rule, Frank, and now one of these little darlings has to pay. Which one will it be? The boy or the girl? I'll let you choose."

I slapped a hand over my mouth to keep Stewart from hearing me cry out. That would just give him more ammunition.

Frank's fist clenched so hard, his skin went white. "I'll give you another five million dollars if you let them both go right now."

"Fifteen million dollars? I'll think about it."

The line went dead.

"Oh my god, he's going to kill them. I know he is, Frank. He's going to kill our baby."

I knew I had grown a little hysterical when Frank grabbed me by the arms and gave me a good shake. "He's not, Henry. I won't let him."

"How can you stop it?" I frowned when Frank grimaced. "Frank?"

He gave a slight shake of his head before looking at the detective. "Is it alright if I take Henry back to his room to lie down? I think this is getting too overwhelming for him."

"Yes, of course."

Frank didn't say anything as he led me out of the room, but he gestured for Martino to follow us as we passed him. When we reached my bedroom, Frank led me over to the bed and pushed me down onto the mattress.

"Frank, wha—" I snapped my mouth closed when Frank held up his hand.

Something was going on. I just had no idea what it was. When Martino stepped into the room, Frank told him to close the door. Once the door was closed, Frank pushed a hand through his hair and then turned to look at me.

"Okay, look," Frank said, "there is someone we can call that might be able to help us track Stewart down, but once we ring that bell, we can't unring it."

Huh?

"Are you sure you want to do this, Frank?"

"You heard him, Martino," Frank said. "He's threatening to kill one of the kids and we have no guarantee that he won't kill them both once he gets the money."

"Yeah, but—"

"He's threatening to kill my daughter, Martino," Frank snapped. "Do you get that?"

"He doesn't know which kid is yours, Frank."

I know emotions were high, but the rage that suddenly flooded every pore of my body was almost mind—numbing. I jumped up from the bed and barreled into Martino, slamming him into the wall. He was bigger than me, but I was pissed.

"Stewart left the choice up to us. Which kid should he kill, Martino? Frank's daughter or your son?" I knew I had no right to give away Ryan's secrets, but the situation was dire. I hope Ryan understood when he learned about the can of worms I'd just opened. "Since you seem to think this is so easy, you pick."

Martino's confusion was almost amusing. "My son?"

"Yeah, remember that one night stand you had with Ryan all those years ago? You know the one where you didn't tell Ryan you were married until after you fucked him? Well, guess what? It's a boy." I grinned maliciously. "So, which one should we tell Stewart to kill? Hmm?"

Martino's brow furrowed. "My son?" he asked again. "Arty is my son?"

"Yes, Arturo is your son."

"Why wouldn't Ryan tell me?"

"Because you're an idiot." I pushed away from Martino and walked over to sit on the side of the bed. I drew in a deep breath. "I had no right to tell you and Ryan is going to be pissed that I did, but you need to understand what is at stake here. You can't choose who lives and dies here. One kid is not more disposable than the other. They both matter."

"I think Martino's hesitancy comes from the fact that the people we have to call aren't exactly...uh...they aren't..."

"They aren't what?" I snapped. I didn't care if they were the devil themselves. If they could help us find Eva and Arty, I didn't know why they hadn't already been called.

"They're not exactly law abiding citizens, Henry," Martino said. "In fact, they are pretty much the opposite of law abiding."

"My grandmother is from the old country," Frank explained. "She has some contacts over there that have contacts over here that might be able to find Stewart and Trevor."

"If they can find our kids, I don't see the problem here."

"Favors like this aren't free," Frank said.

"So, offer them the money you have set aside to pay Stewart." Seemed simple enough to me.

"Not sure they'll want money." Frank grimaced as if he has a bad taste in his mouth. "They usually want favors in return for favors, and that opens us up to a minefield of problems."

"I don't care," I spat out.

Frank glanced at Martino, who nodded. He sighed as he pulled his cell phone out of his pocket, dialed, and then held the phone to his ear. "*Nonna*, this is Francesco. I need you to—" His eyebrows lifted. "You did?" He glanced at Martino. "She already called them. They have men out searching for Stewart now."

I smiled. "I always did like her."

"Yes, *Nonna*?" Frank said as he held the phone back to his ear. He nodded a couple of times before hanging up and looking at me. "I've been informed if I don't get my head out of my ass—her words—and bring you and Eva home where you belong, I'm might as well not come home."

I chuckled.

Frank looked at his brother. "You're basically screwed. She knows about Arturo."

"How?" Martino asked. "I just found out."

"I doubt there is much that gets past that woman," I said. I'd only spent a small amount of time in the Galeazzi household, but some of my favorite memories were having coffee with Eva in her indoor garden.

There was a knock at the bedroom door. Martino reached over and pulled it open. It was one of the officers. He glanced between all of us before his eyes settled on Frank. "The detective would like to see you, sir."

Frank instantly started out of the room. I got up to follow him. No way in hell was I being left behind if something was going on. I ran to keep up because Frank was walking very fast. When we reached the main room, the officer directed Frank to the door.

"He's out front."

Frank headed for the door. When I started after him, he pointed to the floor. "You stay here."

"Frank."

"Please, baby." Frank pressed a hand against my shoulder, keeping me from going out the door. "Let me see what the detective wants. As soon as I know anything, I'll let you know."

Tears prickled at the corners of my eyes. "Frank."

"Please, baby?"

My shoulders slumped and I nodded. Tension and anxiety balled together in my gut. I jerked when I felt someone come up behind me until I realized it was Martino.

"It's going to be okay, Henry."

I hoped so, but I wasn't holding my breath. Mostly because there was no air left in my lungs. I just couldn't seem to inhale enough oxygen. It didn't help that my heart was beating so fast it was about to leap right out of my chest.

"Henry!"

"That's Frank," I whispered as I darted for the front door. I made it out the door and as far as the front porch before I spotted Frank. I sank down onto the steps, unable to take another step. The sobs I'd been trying so hard to hold in broke free and tears began streaming down my cheeks.

Frank had tears on his own cheeks as he walked toward me, holding a kid in each arm. He was surrounded by police officers, one on each side and two behind him. The detective in charge of the kidnapping case was walking with him, talking wildly on his phone.

Frank stopped several feet from me and squatted down on the ground. "Go to Daddy, Eva."

She raced into my waiting arms. I hugged her as tight as I could before looking up at Frank. "Thank you." The words were inadequate, but they were all I had.

He'd given me my little girl back.

Chapter Twenty One

~ Frank ~

"How?" Henry asked.

I was kind of wondering that myself. "The officer said they just walked up to the house."

Henry lifted Eva up into her arms before walking down the steps to me. He reached over and brushed the hair back from Arty's eyes. "Hey, little man, how are you?"

"I want Daddy," Arty said as he burrowed into my chest.

"I know," Henry replied. "But Daddy was really tired so he went to see some friends and take a nap. Maybe we can go see him in the morning."

"Is it because of Daddy's booboo?"

Damn, Arty's words meant the kids had seen Ryan either shot or lying on the floor after he'd gotten shot. That was not a memory I wished either of them to have.

"Yes," Henry said as he shot me a look. "It's because of Daddy's booboo."

"Daddy, Daddy." Eva tugged on Henry's shirt. "That man, he told me to give this to you when he dropped us off at the park." She held out a folded piece of paper.

Geez, the park? They had walked here all the way from the park? Granted, it was only two blocks away, but they were just little kids.

Henry leaned down and set Eva on her feet before opening the paper. His brow furrowed as he read whatever was written there. "Frank."

"What's it say?"

"It's a note from Trevor. He says he never agreed to kidnap any kids, that it was all Stewart's idea. He says he's washing his hands of the whole thing. He's not going to prison for anyone, not even Stewart."

"Did he happen to mention where Stewart might be?"

Henry shook his head.

Well, at least we got the kids back.

"Martino, call Papa and have him arrange some people to...Martino?"

Martino was standing there staring at Arty as if he'd never seen a four year old kid before. There was a surprising sheen in his brown eyes.

"Hey." I waved my hand in front of his face to get his attention.

Martino jerked as if he'd just been electrocuted. "What?"

"Can you hold Arty while I call Papa? I want him to send some men down here to keep an eye on the kids until Stewart and Trevor are found."

"You want me to hold him?"

"He won't bite you, Martino."

"He might," Henry said. "He bit Eva last week when she wouldn't give him a toy he wanted."

"I stand corrected." I didn't give my brother a chance to protest. I just dumped Arty into his arms. He could either catch him or watch him fall to the ground.

Luckily, Martino caught him.

"Let's go inside. I don't want you all out here on the street." We might have the kids back, but I couldn't shake the feeling that this wasn't over.

Henry picked Eva up again and hurried inside, Martino right on his heels. I waited until they had walked away before turning to the detective. "What happened?"

"The kids just walked up to the yard," the man replied. "One of the officers spotted them and rang the alarm."

"Did they see who dropped the kids off?"

"No, but I sent some officers back to the park to look for any security cameras that might be in the area. If we can get some good footage, we might be able to see what kind of car this guy was driving and then identify him."

"I think it was Trevor Franklyn. He gave a note to Eva when he dropped them at the park and told her to give it to Henry. He said he never signed up for kidnapping kids and he was washing his hands of the entire situation."

"Do you have that note?"

"Henry has it."

"I'll need it."

I nodded. "I'll get it from Henry, but first I need to make a phone call." When the detective raised an eyebrow at me, I said, "Now that the kids are home, I want to arrange some security for them until these idiots are caught."

The detective nodded. "I can assign some officers, but I'm not sure how long they would be able to stay, so that's not a bad idea. You might also talk to Mr. Warner about upgrading his security around here. A ten year old with a nail file could break into that place."

If I had anything to say about it, Henry and Eva wouldn't be staying here long enough for that to be a problem. I wanted them home with me.

Once the detective walked away, I pulled out my phone and dialed my father. "Papa, its Francesco."

"Any news?"

"We have the kids, but Trevor and Stewart are still out there."

"Are they okay?"

"They look okay, a little scared, but I don't think they were harmed. Trevor dropped them off at a park two blocks from here."

"Well, at least they're home safe."

"And that's kind of what I needed to talk to you about. I need some security for them until Trevor and Stewart are caught."

"Say no more. I'll call our security guy and see if he has anyone out here that can help out for awhile."

"Thank you, Papa."

"Has Henry agreed to let us meet her yet?"

I winced, not wanting to hurt my father, but not really knowing that answer to his question either. "No, not yet. I don't even think he's thinking about it at the moment. Having Eva kidnapped tore him apart and that's been all he's been able to concentrate on."

Bellino sighed. "I suppose I can understand that. Your Mama and I would have been beside ourselves if something had happened to one of you."

I could understand that sentiment and I'd barely had a chance to say two words to my own daughter. I needed to change that. "I need to go, Papa. I'll let you know if anything changes."

"Alright, I'll let your Mama know Eva is safe and get some security out to you."

"You might want to let Nonna know the kids are safe, too. I called her earlier and asked her to talk to some of her contacts in the old country."

"Oh, son." I could hear the disappointment in his voice.

"I had to, Papa," I insisted, hoping he would understand. "This is my little girl we're talking about, and Stewart was threatening to kill her. I couldn't let that happen."

"No, of course not. I just...You know they are going to want something in return."

"And I'll give them whatever they want if it means my little girl is home safe in her own bed." I reached back and rubbed at the tension knotting the muscles at the back of my neck. "Besides, Nonna had already called them by the time I called her. Maybe whatever favor they ask for won't be so bad since the request came from her."

I could hope anyway.

"Call me if you hear anything," Bellino said. "I'll do the same."

"Thank you, Papa." I hung up and slid my phone back into my pocket. I rested my hands on my hips and tilted my head back to stare up into the night sky for a minute. My relief that the kids had been returned was great, but the threat was still there and I was at a loss as how to fix this mess.

That might actually be what angered me the most. I was always able to fix things, but I was starting to realize that throwing money at this situation was not going to solve it for me. Money is what got us into this mess in the first place.

"Mr. Galeazzi," an officer called out as he stepped onto the porch. "He's calling again."

I took off running for the house. I glanced around as soon as I got inside. "Where are Henry and the kids?"

"I had Henry take the kids to the bedroom when the phone rang," the detective said. "I didn't think it was a good idea for the kids to hear this. There's an officer in there with them."

"No, you're right." I walked to the table. "Okay, everyone ready?"

I received several nods so I hit the connect button on the cell phone. "Stewart."

"Is the jet here?" Stewart asked.

"It is," I replied. My eyes rounded a bit as I realized Stewart didn't know we had the kids back. I glanced at the detective, who made a motion with his hand for me to keep talking. "It's parked at a private hanger at the airport, fueled and ready to go wherever you want."

"And the money?"

"Ready to be wired to your account when we get the kids."

"No, no, that's not how this is going to work. I get the money and then you get the brats."

"What guarantee do I have that you won't harm them once you get the money?"

"None."

Asshole.

"Why are you doing this, Stewart?"

Stewart snorted. "For the money, of course."

"This can't just be about the money. How did you even know about my kid? I just found out a couple of days ago myself."

"You always were an idiot." Stewart's voice hardened ruthlessly. "I knew Henry was pregnant since right after you kicked him to the curb. I knew, given enough time, you'd go looking for him and I was biding my time until you did."

"Why do you hate me so much? What did I ever do to you?" That's what I didn't understand. I didn't like the guy, but I had never been outright rude to him. "Why kidnap my kid?"

"Because I want you to suffer the way you made me suffer," Stewart spat out. "I want your entire family to suffer with the knowledge that you couldn't save your kid, just like I couldn't save Jack."

Jack?

I glanced across the room to Martino, whose face at turned pasty white as he stared down at the phone like it was a snake coiled and ready to bite him. "You mean Jack White?"

"Jack Marcum, my brother," Stewart shouted. "He was my brother, and your family destroyed him. He was ostracized from everyone and everything after Martino made a fool of him. He couldn't get a job. He couldn't get a loan. He couldn't get anything. He died penniless and alone."

Jack's death was news to me, and I could see from Martino's dropped jaw that it was news to him as well.

"I'm sorry to hear that Jack died, but we didn't do anything to him. He did it to himself when he pretended to be someone he wasn't." I cocked my eyes a little and smirked. "Kind of like you did when you said you were carrying Martino's child so you could trap him into marriage."

I was testing out a theory here, but if I was right, it would clear up a lot of things for Martino.

"Your family is so desperate for the next generation of little Galeazzis that they'll jump at any little chance to continue the family line."

I watched as one of the technicians pumped his fist and then waved the detective over. The detective leaned in close to the screen before pulling out his cell phone and walking into the next room.

A moment later, he came out and walked over to me. "Keep him talking," he mouthed.

I nodded.

The detective made a beeline for the front door, several officers following behind him. I walked around the table until I could see the screen and then grinned. They'd pinpointed Stewart's location.

"Is that why you lied, Stewart?" I asked.

"I didn't lie."

"You were never carrying Martino's kid and you know it. I know it, you know it, everyone knows it, even Martino. Why do you think he divorced your skanky ass?"

Maybe that was too much.

"Skanky ass?" Stewart screamed into the phone. "I'll show you skanky ass."

Even through the phone I could hear Stewart's heavy footsteps. "Trevor, where are—what did you do?"

I jerked when two gunshots rang out.

A moment later, Stewart's voice came back on the line. "I guess we're back to ten million dollars now."

Wait.

"You shot one of the kids?"

When everyone in the room turned to look at me, I shrugged. I knew when this conversation had started that Stewart didn't know we had the kids back, but I was starting to think that he didn't know Trevor had returned them to us.

And I was pretty sure that Trevor had just paid for that mistake with his life.

"Pay me another five million and I'll tell you which one is left."

This guy really was an idiot.

"I'm not going to pay you one single cent until I get proof of life." That should put a bee in his bonnet.

"Maybe I'll just shoot the other one."

"No!" I don't know why I shouted that. It wasn't like he was actually going to kill one of the kids. He didn't have them anymore. Maybe it was instinct. "Get me proof of life, let me talk to the kid, and I'll send the money."

"I'll think about it."

I blew out a breath when the line went dead. I pushed my hand through my hair. "I hope I never have to deal with that idiot again."

The phone rang again.

"Fuck me," I whispered before reaching down to hit the connect button.

Stewart sounded as if he was running. He was panting heavily, his rapid footsteps echoing through the phone. "You fucking bastard!" Stewart shouted. "I will end you, and every member of your family."

I heard a couple of distant shouts, a gunshot, and then the phone went dead. I glanced at the technician. "Did they get him?"

"Hold on, I'm checking." The man quickly dialed a number and spoke to someone on the phone. "The detective said that Stewart got away, but one of the officers winged him. They also found Franklyn in a small room at the back of the house. He's been shot."

"Damn it!" I slapped my hand down on the table. "Martino, call Papa and warn them to tighten their security. Stewart is desperate. There's no telling who he might go after."

Martino nodded and then pulled out his cell phone as he walked away.

"Let me know when the detective gets back," I told the technician. "I need to go check on the kids."

I walked down the hallway without saying another word and then opened the door to the kids' room. I smiled when I saw Henry curled up with a kid on each side of him as he read them a story. It looked as if the kids had fallen asleep.

"Hey."

Henry smiled up at me. "Hey." His voice was soft and quiet as he spoke to me.

I spoke in the same quite voice when I asked, "How are they?"

"A little clingy, but that's to be expected."

I'd be a little clingy, too, if I'd been kidnapped and watched someone I care about get shot.

"How are you?" I asked.

Henry shrugged, which told me nothing and everything.

"Once those guys are asleep, why don't you come on out? I have some news." Not much news, but I wanted to keep Henry in the loop.

Henry glanced down. "I think they are asleep, but I may need help getting out of here."

Easy enough.

I walked over, leaned over Arty and picked Henry up in my arms. Arty and Eva both grumbled a little until they wiggled closer and touched each other, and then they fell back to sleep. I set Henry on his feet and then grabbed the blanket at the end of the bed and pulled it up to cover both of them.

When I turned toward Henry, he had tears in his eyes.

"What's wrong?"

Chapter Twenty Two

~ Henry ~

"You're very good at that."

Frank frowned. "At what?"

I smiled. "At taking care of children."

Frank glanced back toward the bed. When he turned toward me again, his cheeks were flushed. "I didn't want them to get cold."

Frank probably didn't realize it, but simple little things like that were what made good parents. Granted, I hadn't been doing this very long and I was no expert, but it seemed pretty straight forward to me.

"What did you want to talk to me about?"

Frank nodded to the door. "Let's go talk out in the hallway. I don't want to wake the kids."

I turned and headed for the hallway then stopped and turned as soon as I was through the doorway. Frank stepped out and closed the door behind me. I expected him to start talking. I didn't expect him to draw me into his arms.

I wasn't against the idea.

I heard his heartbeat when I laid my head against his chest. It was a steady beat, rhythmic. I liked it. Not only did it tell me that Frank was alive, but it told me that he was holding me close enough to hear it.

"We're going to make it, you know," Frank whispered against the side of my head. "Here pretty soon, we're going to announce our engagement to the world and then start looking for a house and—"

I leaned back. "Start looking for a house?"

"Your life is here, Henry. Eva's life is here. I don't want to take you away from that."

"But I thought your work was on the East Coast?"

"Technically, it is, but remember that meeting we had when I first got here?"

I nodded.

"We're expanding our business to this coast." Frank shrugged. "Someone has to run it. Might as well be me, especially since I have family here."

"So does Martino."

"Yeah, but I'm not sure he's ready for that yet."

"And you are?"

Frank's grin was deliciously sexy. "I'm ready for anything and everything you could possibly throw my way."

"Then you'd better be ready for the pregnancy test because we didn't use protection last night and your little swimmers seem to be quite potent where I'm concerned."

I felt Frank's quick intake of breath more than I saw it. I was too busy watching his eyes widen. I chuckled. "Bet you weren't thinking about that, were you?"

"Actually, I've been thinking about it a lot," Frank admitted. "I missed so much with Eva. I don't want to miss anymore."

My eyebrows lifted in surprise. "You want more kids?"

"Yeah, don't you?"

I'd actually never thought about it. I'd always been too busy taking care of the one I already had to consider having more, but I wasn't against the idea. "So, a positive test wouldn't be the end of the world?"

"No, *amore mio*. It would not. I'd just like us to do it together this time, and that means getting married and finding a house to live in for all of us."

I wasn't against that idea either.

"So, what did you need to tell me?" My stomach clenched when the happy smile on Frank's face faded. "I'm not going to like it, am I?"

"Well, the good news is that Trevor was shot, but he's alive. He's at the hospital, but he's been taken into custody."

"Trevor?"

"Looks like Stewart shot him in a fit of rage when he found out Trevor released the kids. The police were able to trace the last phone call. When they got there, there was some shots fired and they think one of them nicked Stewart."

I purposely widened my eyes. "They think?"

"He got away."

"And went where?"

"We don't know, baby." Frank's hand brushed over the side of my face. "The police will find him and in the meantime, I had my father call in some of his security guys to keep us all safe. They should be here soon."

"Did you think to put someone on Ryan?"

Frank stared, his expression showing complete surprise.

"You might want to do that since Ryan is as involved in this mess as the rest of us. Remember, Stewart was the one who took pictures of us five years ago and tried to convince you we were having an affair. He also knows Ryan is injured and most likely to be in the hospital or dead. It wouldn't be too hard to find him."

"Fuck!" Frank pulled out his cell phone and dialed. "Papa, I need you to put a guard on Ryan Jones' room. He's at—" Frank frowned. "What's the name of the hospital, baby?"

"Harborview Medical Center."

"Did you hear that, Papa? Harborview Medical Center." Frank nodded. "Yes, okay, I'll let you know if we hear anything." He hung up and slid his phone back into his pocket. "Papa is going to have someone sent to watch over Ryan until he comes home from the hospital."

"Thank you."

"We'll make sure everyone is protected until Stewart gets caught."

"Are you hungry?" I asked. "I could cook you something."

"I could order something." Frank glanced down the hallway toward the living room. "There are a lot of people here. We should probably feed them, too."

I hadn't thought of that.

"Pizza?" I asked. "There's a really great pizza joint a couple of blocks away."

Frank pulled his wallet out of his pocket, opened it up, and handed me his credit card. "Why don't you order for everyone? Whatever you think they would like. I'm going to go talk to the detective about putting someone on Ryan until security gets there."

"Okay, anything specific you like?"

"Meat."

I chuckled. "Somehow I knew that."

Frank seemed like a meat kind of guy.

I took his credit card and walked into the kitchen to grab the house phone and the take out menu for the pizza place. I quickly counted the number of people in the house and calculated how many pizzas we would need and ordered several different kinds.

Frank was standing talking to one of the officers when I walked back into the main room and handed him back his credit card. "Where's Martino?"

The man wasn't in the room.

"He went up with the officer assigned to Ryan's room to sit with him," Frank said. "I think he's worried about him."

Huh. It was going to be interesting when those two finally sat down and talked to each other. Unlike me, Ryan had gotten in touch with Martino when he found out he was carrying. After Martino told him he was lying and the kid wasn't his, I couldn't blame the man for being angry.

You didn't entice a man, sleep with him, and then inform him that there was no way they could ever be together because you were married and you were just doing this to get back at your husband and then deny your child.

I would have kicked Martino to the curb, too. If Martino wanted Ryan to have anything to do with him, he was going to have to do some serious kissing up. Ryan was going to be extra pissed when he found out that Martino's ex-husband had been the one to shoot him and then kidnap their son.

He might not ever speak to Martino again.

"I'm going to go sit with the kids. Call me when food gets here."

Frank smiled at me. "Okay."

I leaned up and kissed Frank. It was a light kiss, but it had been a long time since I'd been able to kiss him simply because I was leaving the room, or even felt as if I had that right.

When I got to the kids' bedroom, I carefully let myself in and then shut the door behind me. Something warm spread through my chest when I saw them curled up together. They might be cousins, but they were closer than most siblings.

I nodded to the officer sitting in the chair in the corner and then walked over and stretched out on the side of the bed next to them. I couldn't believe they were back and they were safe. I never wanted to experience the kind of fear I'd felt as I did when Stewart had them.

Between the relief I felt that the kids were safe, the stress of the last twenty-four hours, and the knowledge that Frank was there to keep us safe, I felt my eyelids start to drop. I didn't fight it. Frank said he'd come wake me up when the pizza got here.

* * * *

Something jerked me awake. I inhaled slowly and then lifted my head to peer at the kids. Eva and Arty were both still asleep. I sat up and glanced around, trying to figure out what had woke me up. The room was dark and the officer who'd been sitting in the corner was gone.

I brushed the hair back from my face. I guess when Frank checked on me, he decided to let me sleep. I probably needed it. Hopefully, they had left me some pizza.

I made sure the kids were still asleep and covered and then got up and walked toward the door. I pulled it open and stepped out into the hallway, but before I could take another step, I stopped. Something was off.

It took me a moment to figure out what it was. The lights were out in the hallway and in the room beyond and there was no sound coming from any part of the house. That set off alarm bells in my head.

I became increasingly uneasy as I crept down the hallway toward the living room. The lights being out I could accept, but it was the total lack of sound that really bothered me. I don't think this house had ever been this quiet.

I heard the floor creak and I froze. I'd lived in this cottage for five years. I'd gotten used to where the loose floorboards were located. With two small babies in the place, I kind of had to. The hallway was carpeted. No floorboards, which meant that creak had to come from somewhere in the main room.

A suffocating sensation tightened my throat when I peeked around the corner into the living room and saw everyone passed out. I would have thought they were sleeping, except some of them were on the floor.

I tiptoed back to the bedroom as quickly as I could and let myself back into the room. My eyes darted around the room as I looked for a place to hide the children. I couldn't let them be taken again.

My gaze settled on the large wicker toy box in the corner. It was round, with tall sides, big enough to hold all the toys and several stuffed animals. The first thing I had to do was get rid of the toys.

I pulled open one of the dresser drawers, grabbed the stuffed animals and set them aside, and dumped the smaller toys into the dresser drawer. I shut the drawer and then hurried over to the bed.

I shook Eva awake first and then Arty. I held my finger up to my lips. "We're going to play hide and seek." I motioned for the kids to come with me and then walked over to the basket. One by one, I lifted them in and then gestured for them to sit down.

"Listen to me, if you can be absolutely quiet and not get found, I'll take you all to the burger corner for lunch tomorrow. But you have to stay quiet. You can only come out when I come for you. This is our secret. Okay?"

Eva and Arty nodded.

I grabbed the blanket and a couple of pillows off the bed. I gave the pillows to the kids and covered them with the blanket. I stacked the stuffed animals on top of them. "Don't move," I whispered. "Don't make a sound."

Once I was sure that the kids were hidden, I walked over and opened the window. I thought about sending the kids out the window, but where would I send them? I had no idea who might be waiting out there for them.

I even thought about the three of us sneaking out the window and going for help, but Frank was in the house somewhere and I had to find him. I just prayed this wasn't the stupidest move I'd ever made in my life. It could get the kids killed.

I let myself out of the bedroom again and started down the hallway. When I reached the main room, I squatted down to the first officer I came to and checked his pulse. Thankfully, there was one, and it was strong and steady.

I started to grab his radio off his belt to call for help when I realized whoever might be in the house would hear me as soon as I started speaking. I wasn't about to take the officer's gun. I honestly didn't think I could ever shoot anyone, but I could taze them.

I grabbed the tazer off the officer's belt.

The living room was clear, so I suspected whoever was in the house was in the dining room or the kitchen. I started to slowly move in that direction, stepping over another officer on the floor.

I heard the very distinctive sound of flesh hitting flesh. It was too far away to be the dining room. That left the kitchen...and maybe the laundry room, which was on the other side of the kitchen. It led into the garage.

I cleared the dining room, which meant I could see into the kitchen. It was empty. That left the laundry room and the garage. Fear slid up my spine as I crept through the kitchen, making sure I stayed on the left side of the room. The right side—the side by the sink—had loose floorboards.

I heard someone talking, their voice becoming louder the closer I got to the laundry room entrance. When I reached the entrance, I flattened myself against the wall, drew in a bolstering breath, and then peeked around the corner.

There was no one there.

Chapter Twenty Three

~ Henry ~

I clenched my jaw in frustration. My nerves were starting to fray. I didn't really want to run into whoever was here, but I had a burning need to find out who that someone actually was. If there were others working with Stewart that we didn't know about, we were screwed.

I also wanted to find Frank. I hadn't seen him in the living room with any of the others and that worried me.

The laundry room had a lot of creaking boards. I wasn't exactly sure how to get through it without someone hearing me. I briefly entertained the idea of going out and coming in through the garage door, but that would be too obvious. Whoever was in there would hear me the second I unlocked the garage door.

There was a washer and dryer on one side and pantry shelves on the other. I leveraged myself between them and used my arms to steady me as I lifted my feet and crab walked along the tops of them. It was slow going, but there were no creaks.

When I got to the other side, I cautiously lowered myself back down to the floor and then plastered myself against the wall. I gripped the tazer tightly and then peeked around the corner. What I saw threw all my careful caution to the wind.

I ran toward Stewart, raising the tazer in the air. I barreled into him and pressed the tazer against his skin over and over again. The man screamed and went down, taking me with him. I tazed him again and again until he stopped moving.

Once I was sure he wasn't going to move, I dropped the tazer and scrambled over to Frank. "Oh, baby." I didn't quite know where to touch him. His face was a bloody mess. One eye was swollen and there was blood dripping from his nose and mouth.

"Un...tie me."

I hurried around behind Frank and untied his hands. As soon as he was free, he slumped forward. I grabbed him before he could fall to the floor and propped him up in the chair. I squatted down in front of him.

"What can I do?" I felt helpless. This sort of situation was outside my knowledge. I didn't know whether to go get the kids, call the cops, help Frank out, or taze Stewart again.

"Make...make sure he's tied up."

Right.

It felt a bit like poetic justice when I grabbed the rope Stewart had used to restrain Frank to the chair to tie his hands behind his back. Stewart's eyelids were fluttering so I knew he wasn't unconscious, so I kept the tazer close at hand in case I'd need it.

"Now what?"

"Kids?"

"They're safe. I hid them before I came in here."

A huff of air came out of Frank.

I smiled through the tears that started flooding my eyes. "They're safe, Frank. I promise."

"You?"

"I'm okay. I'm not hurt at all."

Frank's eyes sparkled with moisture. "He said...he said he hurt you"

"He never touched me."

"C-Can't have anything happen to you."

A loud crash sounded from the front of the house followed by Martino calling out, "Frank? Henry?"

"We're back here, Martino," I called out. "In the garage."

I heard pounding footsteps and then Martino appeared in the doorway. He seemed to take in the scene with a single swipe of his eyes. He growled when he spotted Stewart on the floor and started for him.

I couldn't believe I found myself standing between them. "He's restrained, Martino. You can't touch him."

"Watch me!"

"Martino," Frank whispered in a voice that sounded like it was fading. "Have to take care of kids, Henry. Can't...Can't..."

I cried out when Frank started to fall forward and pushed past Martino to catch him before he hit the floor. A moment later, Martino was there, helping me gently lower Frank to the floor.

"Get something for his head."

I raced into the laundry room and grabbed several towels from the laundry basket. I hurried back into the garage and stacked them under Frank's head. "He needs an ambulance." I didn't think anything was broken, but it wouldn't hurt to have him examined by a doctor.

"The other officers are in the living room trying to revive the others. Go tell them we need an ambulance and someone to take Stewart into custody."

I got up and hurried back into the main area of the house. The place was a flurry of activity. Several of the officers were trying to rouse the ones passed out. One was talking on his cell phone. The detective we'd been dealing with this other time was pacing as he talked on his own phone.

"Detective."

The man looked up when I called out to him, then said something into his phone and hung up. "Mr. Warner. Do you know what happened here?"

I shook my head. "Not totally. Everyone was passed out when I woke up. But I need an ambulance for Frank and someone needs to come take Stewart into custody." I held out the tazer. "I took this off one of your officers. Sorry."

The man gave me a raised eyebrow look as he took the tazer.

"It was better than taking his gun." I flushed just a bit. "I kind of used it on Stewart."

Several times.

"Where is he?"

"In the garage. Stewart was smacking him around when I found them. I tazed Stewart and then used the rope he used on Frank to tie him up."

The detective told a couple of his officers to go take Stewart into custody before assuring me paramedics were already on the way.

"Where were you?" I asked. That wasn't something I had really thought about before, but now it was a burning question. "When I fell asleep, you all were in here waiting for pizza."

"We received word that someone was trying to get to Ryan so I left a few officers here to guard you and raced to the hospital with the others."

"Ryan?" I pressed a hand to my chest. "Is he okay?"

"Yes, we caught the man who tried to get into his room. He said Stewart paid him to get to Ryan and eliminate him if he could, or create a distraction if he couldn't. That's when I suspected Stewart was going to try to go after you guys. I called, but there was no answer so we raced back here." The detective shook his head as he glanced around. "I don't know how this happened."

I didn't either.

"Are any of your men hurt?"

"It doesn't look like it. They're just unconscious."

"If they're not hurt, just unconscious, I'd say it was something they either ate or drank." My eyes settled on the pizza boxes stacked on the table. The lid of the top box was open and the box was empty. "I'd check the pizza."

"Sir." One of the officers came running into the room with a small black canister in his hand. "We found this on the suspect when we searched him."

The detective frowned as he looked it over. "It looks to be some sort of aerosolizable incapacitating agent."

I blinked in confusion. "I'm sorry, aero what?"

"Sleeping gas."

"So, not the pizza?"

"Probably not, but it would be better to get it tested just to be safe."

He didn't have to tell me twice.

Things became pretty chaotic after that. Several ambulances arrived to care for the fallen officers as well as Frank. Stewart was seen to also, since I'd tazed him a number of times, and then taken away in handcuffs.

Morning was breaking by the time Frank walked into my bedroom where I was laying down with the kids. They'd grown anxious every time I tried to leave the room, which was totally understandable, so I'd taken them to my room to sleep in my bed.

"Hey."

"Hey." Frank smiled and then winced as he pressed his finger to his lip. "Ouch."

"You probably shouldn't do that, at least not until your lip heals."

Frank walked over to the side of the bed and stretched out on the mattress, the kids cuddled between us. His eyes sparkled as he stared down at Eva and Arty. "I was kind of hoping the next time I got you into bed that it would be just the two of us, but this is okay, too."

"Everything calm down out there?"

"Yeah, my father's security guys showed up and took over. They want to talk to you tomorrow about some security measures around the house so we can prevent something like this from ever happening again."

"Pretty sure this type of thing doesn't happen often."

"No, but I don't want to take any chances. Once was more than enough."

I could agree with that one.

"Martino went back up to the hospital to sit with Ryan. He doesn't want him to wake up alone and in a strange place."

Hmm. Interesting.

"Maybe they'll be able to work things out so they can at least be friends and Ryan doesn't feel weird about Martino being in Arty's life." That was assuming Martino wanted to be in Arty's life. I had no idea how he felt about kids.

"I'm not even sure Martino has...accepted is the wrong word, but I'm sure this whole situation is surreal for him. I know it was for me when I first found out about Eva, and I was still in love with you. I have no idea how Martino feels about Ryan."

My breath caught. "You still love me?"

Hope pounded in my heart.

Frank's dark eyebrows slammed down over his eyes. "Of course I still love you. Do you think I would be going through all of this if I wasn't?"

"No...Maybe...I Just thought, with Eva and all—"

Frank grabbed my hand and brought it to his lips. "I am over the moon about Eva, saddened that I wasn't there from the very beginning, and angry for letting myself be fooled by Stewart. I am in love with you and have been for five very long years. My feelings didn't change because of what I thought you had done, and that might be why I was so damn angry at you. I felt like you had stabbed me in the heart."

"You know I didn't—"

"I know, baby. I think I always knew. But like you said, I was in the mindset where you were guilty until proven innocent, so when Stewart presented his evidence, it just proved to me I was right."

"What's going to prevent this from happening again?"

"Besides the fact that I trust you, you mean?"

"Do you?"

"Yes, Henry, I do. I should have trusted you before and I didn't." Frank's eyes turned glossy as they went to Eva. "And I will pay for that for the rest of my life. There are memories you have with her that I will never have, and I only have myself to blame for that."

"Frank—"

"I'll give up the money if that's what you want me to do, Henry. I'll donate it all to charity or give it to my family, whatever you want. I'll resign as CEO and get a job as a construction worker again. I'll just be a regular guy."

Francesco Galeazzi would never be a regular guy, but maybe Frank could be.

Frank still had a hold of my hand. I pulled his toward me and pressed a kiss to the top. "How about we see how things go?"

"Do you mean that, Henry?"

"I do."

Frank grinned. "Remember those words."

"Are you going to kiss?"

My mouth dropped open as I glanced down and found two sets of soft brown eyes staring up and me and Frank. I chuckled at the inquisitive look Eva was giving Frank. "We might."

"He looks like me," Eva said.

I felt a warm glow flow through me as I gazed across at Frank, who was staring down at Eva as if she was the most precious treasure in the world, and she was. "That's because he's your daddy."

Chapter Twenty Four

~ Henry ~

"He called again."

I turned away so Ryan couldn't see the smile on my face. "Yeah? And did you talk to him this time?" Martino had called every single day for the last month, ever since Ryan left the hospital.

So far, Ryan had refused to speak to him.

"No, and I'm not going to," Ryan insisted. "He had his chance five years ago and he didn't want it. Why should I give him another one just because he changed his mind?"

"I'm not saying *you* have to, but what about Arty?" I turned to look at my best friend. "You're denying him a chance to get to know his father."

Ryan's lips parted.

"Look, I'm not saying you have to play happy family with him, but Arty does have a right to meet Martino and get to know him. Even as angry as you are at Martino, you know that. Start small. Let him go to the park with you and Arty, or better yet, come to lunch with us and we'll invite Martino along."

"His parents are going to be there," Ryan said. "Do you really think it's a good idea to add in another grandchild?"

"Please?"

"Oh, I see how it is." Ryan laughed. "You want me there as a buffer."

I winced because he was right. This would be the first time I'd seen Frank's parents since they kicked me out all those years ago and I was terrified. Not only was my last meeting with them horrible, but now I was supposed to introduce my daughter to them.

"Maybe if we went together, we could show a united front."

Ryan's eyebrows lifted and I knew he liked that idea.

"It could be fun."

Ryan snorted.

"Okay, it'll be grueling, but we'd be there to support each other. Besides, *Nonna* is going to be there and you'll adore her. She's great." She was one of the main factors in me agreeing to have this lunch. I had missed her something fierce. "She'd be crazy about Arty, especially since you named him after her husband."

I walked over to take Ryan's hands in mine. "Look, you don't have to talk to anyone if you don't want to, not even *Nonna*, but I think you'll want to once you meet her. Besides, you can leave whenever you want. Just give it a shot."

"I'll agree under one condition. Martino has to sign that parenting agreement you had Frank sign."

Uh... "I can ask, but I can't guarantee he'll do it."

"He signs or I don't go. I'm not giving him a chance to take Arty away from me."

That I could understand.

"Let me call Frank." I pulled out my cell phone and dialed my new fiancé. I'd finally accepted his marriage proposal a couple of days ago, which was why we were going to see his parents. "Hey, Frank," I said when the man answered. "I need a favor."

"Anything, *amore mio.*"

"You know, one of these days you're going to say that and I'm going to ask for something really outrageous."

Frank chuckled. "For you, I would do it."

"Keep that thought in mind when I ask you about my favor. Ryan has agreed to come with us so your parents can meet Arty, but he wants Martino to sign that parental agreement Mr. Evans wrote up for us first."

"I see."

Yeah, I didn't think it would be that easy.

The front doorbell rang. Ryan motioned that he would go answer it. I nodded and continued speaking to Frank. If it was for me, Ryan would come get me. "Can you see if Martino would be willing to do that? You can sweeten the deal by letting Martino know that Ryan said he could be there, too."

"That might actually make a difference," Frank said. "Martino has been going out of his mind trying to get Ryan to talk to him."

"Ryan's not doing much better."

"This would cause us all a lot less headaches if those two would just sit down and talk to each other."

"Yeah, maybe, but I can understand where Ryan is coming from."

"And I can understand where Martino is coming from."

I chuckled lightly. "Maybe you can explain it to me later, you know, if we ever get two seconds alone together without your daughter demanding your attention."

Eva had taken to Frank like a duck to water. I was almost jealous of how much time she wanted to spend with him except I knew he was the shiny new toy of the moment and that interest would end as soon as he told her no for the very first time.

It had yet to happen.

"Maybe we can convince Ryan to take Eva for a couple of hours while we go out to dinner or something."

I was really interested in that something. The first week after Stewart was arrested, I refused to be parted from Eva even when we were sleeping. That first night she slept in her own room, I was up and down all night long, checking on her. It took almost another week before I was able to stay in bed all night long.

And Frank had been right there with me every step of the way, but there had not been a whole lot of adult time.

I needed to get laid.

"You still have your hotel suite," I said. He might have been sleeping in my bed every night, but he visited with his family at the hotel. "Maybe Eva and I can come spend the night. I'm sure we can get one of those rollaway cots for her. And after she goes to bed..." I trailed off, letting Frank fill in the blanks.

"I'm liking this idea already."

I grinned even though he couldn't see it. "I thought you might."

"Henry, that detective is here," Ryan said as he walked into the room. "He needs to speak to you."

"Okay, Ryan. Tell him I'll be right there." I waited for Ryan to walk away before saying, "I might be a little late. The detective is here. He needs to speak to me."

"Leave me on speaker. I want to hear what he has to say."

"Okay, hold on." I put my phone on speaker and walked into the living room. "Detective? You needed to see me?"

"Afternoon, Mr. Warner. I just wanted to come by and give you an update on the case."

I wasn't sure I wanted to know what the detective had to come to my house to tell me.

"After Mr. Marcum was processed and put into the system, we started getting phone calls from all over the place. It looks like Mr. Galeazzi wasn't the first person he tried to scam money out of."

Not surprised in the least.

"After he gets tried here, we're shipping him off to California. Texas and Maryland want him, too. If he's found guilty here, he'll still has to serve his time for kidnapping and for the numerous attempted murder charges, but there are a lot of other charges pending. I don't think you have to worry about Stewart Marcum any longer."

"Oh my god, that is so great." I'd feared for ages that he'd get out on bail or something. "What about your men? Did they all recover okay?"

"They did, thank you for asking."

"What about Trevor?" Frank asked. "What's going to happen to him?"

"We're currently holding Mr. Franklyn as an accessory since he gave confidential information to Mr. Marcum, but we're still trying to determine how much he had to do with everything. He is wanted in Texas, however, so once we're done with him, he'll be extradited there."

"Can he get out on bail?" Frank asked, but I kind of wanted to know that as well.

"Technically, yes, but his bail has been set at five million dollars, and unless you want to bail him out, he has no other funds. All of his assets have been frozen by the FBI as they are handling the investigation since this was a kidnapping, and that's a federal offense."

I couldn't help thinking we should have gotten the FBI involved earlier.

"I'm not sure if this will mean anything to you or your brother, Mr. Galeazzi, but we did find out some information on Jack Marcum. He committed suicide after he became broke and destitute. We also believe he was on drugs due to the autopsy they did at the time."

I didn't think that was going to make Martino feel any better. He might have been pissed at the guy and feeling betrayed, but I was sure Martino never wished him dead.

"Several of the states who contacted us had information on him," the detective continued. "Your brother was just one in a long line of men he tried to con money out of. His brother and he were working together, and then they brought Mr. Franklyn into their little scheme. You know where it went from there."

Unfortunately, we all did.

I smiled and held out my free hand. "Thank you for coming to let us know, detective."

I shook the man's hand and then showed him to the door before holding the phone to my ear again. "So, did you get all of that?"

"Yes," Frank replied. "I'll inform my family before you get here so you don't have to."

I wasn't sure I liked that idea or not. If he told them beforehand, they were going to have gold digger on the brain. If he did it after I arrived, same thing, but I'd be there for them to turn their anger on. Either way, I was kind of screwed.

"Maybe we need to plan this for another day?"

"It'll be fine, Henry. I promise. My parents are very sorry for the way they treated you."

That did not make me feel any better.

"Please give them a chance."

I huffed. "Fine, but the first time they start in about money, I'm done. I'll leave."

"Agreed, as long as you take me with you."

I grinned. "Agreed."

* * * *

"I'm going to throw up," I whispered, hoping only Ryan could hear me. Little ears and all that. "I swear I am."

"You dragged me along on this circus," Ryan countered. "I get to throw up first."

Yeah, okay, Ryan might have it a bit worse than me. Frank actually wanted me. The jury was still out on Martino.

When the elevator doors to the penthouse suite opened, Frank was waiting for us. I felt a little better when I saw him. I was even happier when Eva squealed and ran into his arms. Frank grabbed her and swung her up into the air before hugging her. He locked her into his side before reaching for me and planting a kiss on my lips.

"You ready for this?" he asked.

"No," I whimpered.

Ryan snorted. "He's five seconds from spewing."

Frank raised an eyebrow.

"Yeah, so, I'm a little nervous."

"No reason to be nervous, *amore mio.* We're just going to have a little meet and greet and then some lunch. And I'll be with you every step of the way, whether we stay or go."

"Yeah, okay." I drew in several slow breaths to calm myself then shot Frank a wobbly smile. "Okay, let's do this."

"Are you sure?"

I wasn't sure, but the longer I pushed it out, the more time I'd have to worry about it. It was just better to get this over and done with. "Yes, I'm sure."

Ryan snorted again. "I'm glad one of us is."

I leaned over to him and whispered, "Use Arty as a shield. They can't jump you if you're holding the kid."

Ryan laughed, which was what I had been hoping for.

"Martino is here, but he did sign the parenting agreement," Frank said. "I have a notarized copy if you want it."

Ryan shook his head. "Not right now. I'll get it from you before I leave."

"You guys ready?"

I nodded. Ryan shrugged.

Frank squatted down and set Eva on her feet before grabbing her hand and then Arty's. "I have some people for you to meet, okay? If you feel uncomfortable at any time, you just tell me or your dads. Understand?"

Eva and Arty nodded.

"Okay." Frank stood, still holding their hands, and started walking into the main room. Ryan and I followed after.

The ball in my throat thickened when I spotted Frank's parents sitting on the couch, Martino standing behind them. His father was sitting ramrod straight. His mother had a handkerchief held to her mouth and tears in her eyes. Martino's expression was blank until he spotted Ryan and then a mix of emotions slid across his face. Hope, despair, need, and a little bit of anger.

When I spotted the one person I really wanted to see, I let out a little cry of joy and raced across the floor to give *Nonna* a hug. She was waiting for me with open arms.

"It's about time you came home, young man."

I laughed as I hugged her. "I missed you, *Nonna*."

"I missed you, too, son. Now, where is this little angel I've been hearing about?"

I turned and held out my hand. "Eva, come here. I have someone I want you to meet."

Eva gave her father a kiss on his cheek and then ran over to me. I sat down on the couch next to *Nonna* and wrapped my arm around Eva when she reached me. "Poppet, this is Eva Galeazzi, your papa's grandmother. We call her *Nonna* and I bet if you asked real nice, she'd let you call her *Nonna*, too."

Eva leaned toward me and whispered loudly as only a child could. "She has my name, Daddy."

I grinned when Eva laughed. "Actually, you have her name. You were named after her just as Arty was named after *Nonna's* husband."

Eva glanced around. "Where is he? I don't see him."

"Oh, child, he's here." Eva's voice was a little shaky. "But he's an angel now so you can't see him, but he will always look over you and Arturo."

Eva was mesmerized by *Nonna* as I knew she would be. She hadn't had a grandparent figure in her life since Ryan's grandmother passed away. When Eva stepped closer to *Nonna* and looked up at her, I held my breath, waiting to see what would happen.

"Do you miss him?" Eva asked.

"I do," *Nonna* admitted. "I miss him very much."

"Is that why you're crying?"

"Some, but most of these are happy tears because I get to meet you and Arturo. I've been waiting a very long time to meet both of you."

"Does Arturo look like him because I look like my daddy and my papa?"

"I'm not sure."

I knew everyone had to be holding their breath. I was. It was also almost silent in the large living room.

Eva turned and ran over to grab Arty's hand and then pulled him over to *Nonna.* "This is *Nonna.* I think she's like a grandma, but older. I have her name and you have her husband's name so you probably look like him."

"Would you like to see a picture of him?" *Nonna* asked.

Eva and Arty both nodded.

"Francesco, get my bag off the end of my bed."

Eva leaned in and whispered again. "That's my papa."

Nonna smiled. "I know," she whispered. "Your papa is my grandson, which makes you my great-granddaughter." Not to leave the other child out, *Nonna* turned to Arty and tapped his chest. "And you, young man, are my great-grandson."

"Is that why we can call you *Nonna?*" Eva asked.

Oops. She was supposed to ask. "Oh, Eva—"

"You are a very smart young girl," *Nonna* said. "That is exactly why."

Frank came back into the room and handed *Nonna* her bag. She opened it up and pulled out a small locked metal case. I saw that it was a photo holder when she opened it. *Nonna* picked the very first picture off the stack and held it out to the two small four year olds.

"This is Arturo before he became an angel. You don't look much like him here, but he was very old in this picture." She reached for the next picture. "But this one, you look just like him in this picture. He was around your age when this photograph was taken."

I hadn't realized how much Arty looked like Frank's grandfather until I saw the picture *Nonna* was holding. He looked more like Arturo than he did Martino. There was no denying the family resemblance.

"Daddy, look." Arty grabbed the picture and ran back to Ryan, who dropped down to one knee to see what his son wanted to show him. "Look, Daddy, I look like an angel."

They both did.

Chapter Twenty Five

~ Frank ~

So far so good.

Henry and my parents hadn't gone for each other's throats, but they weren't really talking, either. I decided I needed to do something to break the tension in the room before it smothered us all.

"Eva, come here." I held out my hand to my daughter. When she ran over and took my hand, I walked her over to my parents. I squatted down next to her. "Eva, this is my mama and papa." I smiled at my parents. "Mama, Papa, this is my daughter, Eva Maria Warner."

Eva leaned into me, laid her head on my shoulder, and ducked her head, peering up at my parents through her long lashes. I'd only known her a handful of weeks, and I'd seen her do a lot of things, but I'd never seen her be shy with anyone.

"Hello, Eva," my mother said. "I'm your grandmother."

Eva's brow furrowed. "Is that different than *Nonna*? Cause she said I was her great-granddaughter."

"In a way it is. I'm your father's mother and this is his father." She gestured to the man sitting at her side. "*Nonna* is his mother and Arturo was his father."

"Do I call you *Nonna*?" Eva asked.

"Oh no, I haven't earned that title yet. You can call me Nana."

I smiled when Eva started gravitating toward my mother. I had hoped it wouldn't take long. I wanted my family whole, all of them. If I could get Eva and my parents together, I might be able to get Henry and them together as well.

I felt a presence beside me and glanced over to find Henry standing next to me. He reached down and settled his hand on my shoulder, but didn't say a word.

My stomach churned with anxiety, not knowing what was going to happen. Henry could easily get his revenge for how my parents had kicked him out after welcoming him into the family fold. Or he could let his anger and animosity go. It really could go either way, and Henry wouldn't be the guilty party either way he went.

"Mr. Galeazzi," Henry said. "Mrs. Galeazzi. It's good to see you both."

I knew he was lying, but he was being polite about it. Still, I saw my father flinch at the cold, but polite address. Henry used to call him Papa.

"We're planning a day out tomorrow. We're going to go to the zoo and then to the park," Henry said. "Would you like to join us?"

That was quite the olive branch Henry was holding out.

It was up to my parents to take it.

"Oh yes," Eva said. "Daddy and Uncle Ryan are making us a picnic and everything. You have to come, Nana. And *Nonna*, too. Uncle Ryan said he'd make cupcakes if we put all of our toys away before bed. I want one with pink frosting. Arty likes blue, but he's a boy and boys like blue."

She was obviously oblivious to the tension in the room.

My mother chuckled. "I like pink, too, and I would love to go to the zoo and the park with you."

I almost breathed out a sigh of relief when my mother accepted Henry's invite. It wasn't the reunion I truly wanted, but it was a start of mending the fences between my parents and Henry. I knew it would take time for true forgiveness to happen, but this was a sign it would eventually.

Eva squealed and raced over to Arty and started talking with him faster than I could keep up. I purposely widened my eyes when I glanced up at Henry. "I think my ears are bleeding."

Henry chuckled. "You ain't seen nothing yet. That's her happy noise. Wait until she throws a temper tantrum."

When I heard a small snort, I turned toward my mother. I could see from the laughter dancing in her eyes and the way she was holding her handkerchief to her lips that she was trying hard not to laugh.

"What?" I asked.

She moved the handkerchief, but her lips were pressed tightly together as she shook her head. She still looked as if she was trying not to laugh.

"You've been known to shatter glass when you were her age," my father said. "Lost one of my best drinking glasses that way."

I was doomed.

I glanced up at Henry again. "Sorry."

Henry grabbed my hand and pressed it against his abdomen. "This one better take after me or I'm not doing this again."

I sucked in a quick breath. "Yeah?"

Henry smiled and nodded. "Yeah."

I let out a loud whoop, grabbed Henry around the waist, and spun him around. By the time I set Henry down on his feet again, Ryan was standing there with Arty, Martino hovering behind them. *Nonna* had moved to sit next to my father, and my mother and father were staring at us looking confused.

Henry shook his finger at me. "No more spinning. Not good."

"Yes, *amore mio*," I whispered. "Whatever you say."

Henry wiggled his eyebrows. "I knew you'd get it eventually."

~ The End ~

Also Available From
Aja Foxx

SHIFTER KINGS
Alpha Knows Best
Savage Bite

SOLDIERS OF FORTUNE
Forgiveness
Reckoning
Absolution

GUARDIANS OF THE PACK
Protecting His Own

GALEAZZI TRILOGY
That One Time
One More Time

SINGLE TITLES
The Rising
Human ~~Vampire~~ Prince
Prince Charming NOT!
How To Summon A Boyfriend

Also Available From
Aja Foxx & Ciena Foxx

WILDE WOLVES
His Unconventional Omega
Denying His Alpha
Lone Wolf
His To Claim

Forgiveness
Soldiers of Fortune 1

His name was Bug. I assumed it was because he was nuttier than a bed bug until he saved me when I was attacked. For reasons known only to him, Bug thought it was his duty to keep me safe. I was the sergeant-at-arms of the Soldiers of Fortune MC. I didn't need saving, but I couldn't bring myself to tell him so, especially not after I discovered he was my mate.

STORY EXCERPT

"Roses red, violets blue, sugar sweet and so is you, but roses wilting, violets dead, sugar lumpy, and so is you head. So is you head. You head. You head. Lumpy you head."

I cracked an eye open and looked up at the man softly singing as he stroked his fingers through my hair. I wasn't exactly sure what was going on. The world around me was a bit fuzzy, all except the man hovering over the top of me.

Pale skin, a thin face with high cheekbones, hollow, sunken eyes, and a wicked looking scar that went from his cheekbone back into his hairline. Long, stringy hair that might have been blond if it hadn't been so matted and dirty. But it was the pale moss green eyes that held my attention the most. There was a world of pain and anguish in those little green orbs.

I frowned when a flower was placed on my cheek. When I went to reach for it, the grungy little man gasped then scurried back several feet. He stayed crouched on the floor, hunkering down as if trying to make himself as small as possible and covering his head with his arms.

"Lumpy, lumpy, lumpy," the man whispered, but maybe he was more of a boy.

I couldn't quite tell.

I started to sit up then groaned when shards of pain sliced through my skull. When I reached up and felt the nice sized egg on the back of my head, I suddenly understood what the man had meant by lumpy.

No wonder my head ached so damn much.

I sank back down onto the cold concrete and closed my eyes. I breathed in through my nose then out through my mouth, trying to calm myself enough to get through the pain slamming into me.

I opened my eyes again when I heard a scraping noise. The man moved closer, once again placing flowers on my face and down my neck, then over my chest as if the last thirty seconds had never happened.

He started chanting that stupid rhythm again.

"What is your name?" I asked.

The man froze. He didn't even blink. He might not have even been breathing.

"What is your name?" I asked again, in the softest tone I knew how to make, which wasn't easy. I didn't exactly have a soft tone, but I didn't want to scare him.

"Bug. I'm Bug. I scurry around and hide in dark, so yeah, I'm Bug. Not bad Bug. Not cockroach Bug. Good Bug." He held up a handful of flower petals. "Maybe ladybug, but not lady. No, no, not lady. Boy Bug. Boy Bug. So, I'm Bug."

Okay then.

"I'm—"

"Bear." Bug nodded and started with the flowers again. "Bear. Bear. Big, bad Bear. Teddy Bear." Bug patted my chest just open the collar of my shirt. "Furry Bear."

Okay, apparently he knew who I was.

"Where are we, Bug?" It was dark and all I could see were shadows cast by a sliver of light coming in through a crack in the wall.

"Hole. Hidey hole. Small little hidey hole." Bug's brow flickered. "No bad guys here. No. No. Safe here. Bug keep Bear safe." Bug shot up and hurried over to the corner. I watched as he dug into a pile of stuff stacked on the floor. It looked like garbage, but what did I know.

When he came back, he set a gun down on my chest then held his closed fist out. When I opened my hand, he dropped a handful of bullets into my palm. "Safe. Yes, Bug keep you safe. No more wilting flowers. No more lumpy."

I moved slowly when I sat up, trying not to scare Bug, but he still scurried out of arm's reach. I checked over the pistol. It wasn't mine. I had no idea who it belonged to.

"Is this your gun, Bug?" For some odd reason, it didn't sit well with me thinking that Bug needed a gun to protect himself.

"No, no." My eyebrows shot up when Bug laughed. "Bug no like guns. Guns hurt. Guns loud. Guns make people go away. Guns bad."

All of that was true.

"Where did you get the gun, Bug?"

"Mmm," Bug hummed to himself as he tapped the side of his head with his fist. "Bad man, bad, bad, bad man. Hurt Lumpy. Hit Lumpy. Make Lumpy bleed. But Bug got him, yes he did. Bug make bad man go away. Bug keep Lumpy safe."

Holy shit!

"Someone hurt me?"

"Mmm," Bug hummed as he nodded.

"And you...made him go away?"

Bug nodded again as he patted his own chest as if proud of himself. "Bug protect Lumpy."

I wasn't thrilled with being called Lumpy, but it seemed like I had something to thank Bug for, so I let it slide. For now. "Where is this bad man, Bug?"

"Alley by bike. Yes, he is. Left him in alley by bike. Bike, bike, big shiny Lumpy bike."

"My bike?" I growled.

Bug hummed.

Well, shit.

The last thing I remember was parking my bike in front of a warehouse where I was supposed to be meeting a contact. I had turned off the engine and climbed off my bike, then nothing but darkness until I woke up with Bug putting flowers on my face.

"Is my bike still in front of the warehouse?" I asked, hoping Bug knew about the warehouse. I'd be pissed if something happened to my bike. I'd spent four years customizing that damn thing.

"No, no, no." Bug chewed on his thumbnail for a moment. His eyes moved to mine then darted away. "Moved big shiny bike. Hide big shiny bike. Bug protect Lumpy. Bike belong to Lumpy. Bug protect bike."

I just had no idea what to say to that other than, "Thank you, Bug."

The corner of Bug's mouth twitched before lifting just a bit at the corners. "Welcome, welcome, welcome," he sang softly as he tucked a flower into the pocket of my shirt. "Lumpy welcome."

Still wasn't thrilled being called Lumpy.

"I need to get my bike, Bug. Can you take me to it?" I felt as if I was dealing with a small child. Bug was sketchy and jumpy. He chewed on his fingernails a lot. They were practically nubs. "I really need my bike, Bug."

I also needed to check in with Butch. I don't know what happened, but if someone jumped me, I wanted to find the bastard and teach him the error of his ways. Filling my MC President in on who I was going to rip apart before I did it was always a good idea.

I patted my vest down, looking for my phone. I was not happy when I didn't find it. "Bug, did you take my phone."

Bug frowned. "Ring, ring, ring. Not good for Lumpy. Too much noise. Lumpy hurt. Need rest. No noise."

"I need my phone, Bug. I have to call my...uh...boss."

Bug huffed before turning to the pile in the corner. He rooted around for a moment before coming back with my cell phone. "Call boss man," he snapped as he slapped the phone down in my hand. "He not protect Lumpy. He...he...he bad."

I sighed. "He's not bad, Bug. I promise." Well, he was kind of bad. He wasn't exactly a law abiding citizen, thank god, but I trusted him with my life. I needed Bug to trust him, too. "He didn't know I was going to get hurt."

"Jumped. Lumpy get jumped. Bad man with pipe hurt Lumpy. Was waiting behind dumpster for Lumpy." Bug's green eyes grew a little wild. "Bad man wait and wait and wait. Smoke a lot and wait more. Make phone call when Lumpy come then hurt Lumpy."

Holy shit.

About The Author

MM ROMANCE WITH FIERY PASSION

The vicious bite of an enemy, a shout, a cry in the dark. A lover's touch, the whisper of a kiss. A sigh, a groan, heart beating faster, desire surging through a body. Love words spoken in the shadows. The yearning for a soft caress. I'm a writer of fiery passion in all its glorious forms. Paranormal, Contemporary, Sci-Fi, Fantasy, MM Romance books. There is no limit to my imagination.

https://ajafoxx.com/
https://twitter.com/Aja_Foxx
https://www.facebook.com/aja.foxx.69
https://www.amazon.com/Aja-Foxx/e/B07VX6TYJ4

Made in the USA
Las Vegas, NV
08 October 2024